The Everyday Witch

By
Sandra Forrester

BARRON'S

DEDICATION

To Bettye, Joe, and Carolyn—who knew all about the magic of childhood and passed it on to me through their stories.

© Copyright 2002 by Sandra Forrester

All inquiries should be addressed to:
Barron's Educational Series, Inc.
250 Wireless Boulevard
Hauppauge, New York 11788
http://www.barronseduc.com

Library of Congress Catalog Card No.: 2002016317

International Standard Book No.: 0-7641-2220-7

Library of Congress Cataloging-in-Publication Data
Forrester, Sandra.
 The everyday witch / by Sandra Forrester.
  p. cm.
 Summary: On the eve of her twelfth birthday, Beatrice Baily is surprised to find that the decision about her classification as a witch has not been made and that she must first perform a task involving the evil Dally Rumpe.
  ISBN 0-7641-2220-7
  [1. Witches—Fiction.] I. Title.
  PZ7 .F7717 Ev 2002
  [Fic]—dc21
                                        2002016317

PRINTED IN THE UNITED STATES OF AMERICA

9 8 7 6 5 4 3 2

Contents

BAILIWICK

Skull House

Blood Mountain

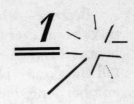

Beatrice Bailey

*T*wilight had come quickly. Streetlights buzzed, then flickered on. A fitful wind snatched up dead leaves from along the curb and sent them skittering down the street. Bare branches clawed at the side of the house like an animal scratching to be let in.

Beatrice Bailey raced up the porch steps, taking them two at a time. She flung open the front door and burst into the hallway, bringing the October chill and the smell of burning leaves with her. The grandfather clock was striking seventeen. A small golden brown bat hanging upside down in the clock case covered its ears with its wings and scowled at the racket.

You wouldn't have noticed the bat in the shadowy hall if you hadn't been looking for it. That's the way it was at the Bailey house—everything seemed perfectly normal on the surface, but when you looked closer, you discovered peculiar things going on. And you noticed, too, that the people who lived in that house weren't as ordinary as they appeared at first glance.

Beatrice—who, at the age of four, had announced that no one was ever to call her Bea or Trixie or anything else besides Beatrice—would be twelve in five days. She was tall and skinny. Her face was skinny, her body was skinny, and her long, blue-jeaned legs were the skinniest of all. Even her hair was skinny—pale red and silky, and *skinny* the way some red hair is. It was cut straight across at the shoulder, with a sweep of bangs that habitually fell into her eyes.

Beatrice blew her bangs aside and placed an armload of books on the hall table so that she could take off her jacket. Just then a huge long-haired mop of a cat—predominantly black, with an occasional dash of orange or white—came padding down the hall. The cat leaped from the floor to the table, sending library books flying.

"Cayenne!"

The cat seemed unfazed by Beatrice's startled cry and began to rub her head against the girl's elbow. Beatrice promptly forgot about the books scattered at her feet and scooped up the cat, who settled like a bag of sand into the crook of Beatrice's arm. Closing green gold eyes that bore a striking resemblance to Beatrice's own, Cayenne began to purr. It was a choppy, rumbling sound, not unlike that of a gasoline engine in need of a tune-up. Although no words were exchanged between girl and cat, there passed between them a communication of deep satisfaction with each other.

Beatrice was doing her math homework at the dining room table when Mr. and Mrs. Bailey came home. They were both tall and skinny like their daughter, and Mrs. Bailey's hair was the same pale red. Mr. Bailey's few remaining hairs were dark, and carefully arranged to cover a wide expanse of pink scalp. The Baileys were dressed in identical khaki pants and forest green jackets with *Bailey Nursery & Garden Center* embroidered across the front.

"Hi, sweetheart." Mrs. Bailey kissed the top of Beatrice's head as she passed through the dining room on her way to the kitchen. She was carrying a tray filled with drooping seedlings.

"Hope you're hungry," Mr. Bailey said, holding up a bag of take-out burgers and fries before following his wife through the doorway.

Beatrice looked up from her homework and sniffed the air. Cayenne, who had been napping inside her mistress's backpack, poked her head out and sniffed, as well. In a flash, they were heading for the kitchen themselves.

Beatrice and her father sat at the table to eat. Cayenne lapped a vanilla shake from a bowl on the floor. Mrs. Bailey ate her dinner standing over the sink. She was spraying a fine mist on the tray of plants as she simultaneously spoke to them and chewed. "You look better already," she assured the seedlings. "With a little care, you'll grow up as strong and glossy as your brothers and sisters."

Mr. Bailey rolled his eyes, and Beatrice gave her father a meaningful look. They continued to eat their burgers and didn't say anything.

Mrs. Bailey glanced at her husband and daughter. "I'll cook tomorrow night. I promise."

Beatrice gave Mr. Bailey another meaningful look. Her mother wasn't much of a cook.

3

"Something healthy," Mrs. Bailey added. "Broccoli, maybe?"

"Well," Mr. Bailey said, and cleared his throat, "as long as you do it the regular way, and don't use mag—"

"Of course not," Mrs. Bailey snapped. Nothing annoyed her more than being reminded of her shortcomings.

"I didn't mean to criticize," Mr. Bailey said gently. "It's just that something awful happens every time you try to use your mag—"

"And you're on a par with Merlin, I suppose."

"No, no, I didn't mean that," Mr. Bailey said hastily. "I gave up long ago trying to use my mag—"

"And a good thing, too," Mrs. Bailey said frostily, "after you nearly blew up the house!"

"I was only trying to light a fire in the fireplace," Mr. Bailey said defensively.

They had just finished dinner, and Beatrice was gathering up burger wrappers and French fry containers, when the doorbell rang. Everyone's head turned toward the sound at the front of the house. A mouse living under the sink took the opportunity to dart out and grab a fry that had fallen to the floor. Cayenne pounced, but the tip of the mouse's tail slipped through her claws and he shot back into his hole.

"I wonder who's at the door," Mrs. Bailey said without much interest, and turned back to her plants.

"I'll go see," Mr. Bailey replied.

Cayenne lay with her nose flattened against the baseboard under the sink, one glittering eye filling the mouse hole. Well out of reach, the mouse strutted back and forth

4

in front of the cat and made squeaking sounds that might have been laughter.

As Beatrice stuffed the remains of dinner into the trash can, Mr. Bailey's voice carried back to her.

"*Be-a-trice*, you have visitors."

Beatrice was surprised. She hadn't expected Teddy or Ollie or Cyrus to stop by. With Fall Break less than two weeks away, their teachers had been piling on the homework and there hadn't been much time to hang out together.

Beatrice bounded out of the kitchen, through the dining room—and then stopped short. She was amazed to see Amanda Bugg, the biggest phony in seventh grade, and Amanda's dimwit boyfriend, Jason Twitchel, standing with her father in the front hall. Beatrice approached them warily.

"Hi, Beatrice," Amanda said brightly. She flipped her long hair back over her shoulder, as she did frequently, ever since a boy in fourth grade had told her how cute she looked when she did that.

Jason slumped beside Amanda with his hands thrust deeply into his pockets, smirking and not looking Beatrice in the eye.

"Why don't you take your friends into the living room?" Mr. Bailey suggested. "Your mother will bring you some snacks."

"I'll bet Amanda and Jason just had dinner," Beatrice said. Her eyes bored into Amanda's face. "You're stuffed, right? Couldn't eat another bite?"

"I could handle a snack," Jason said absently as he peered past her down the hall.

"Refreshments coming right up," Mr. Bailey said.

Beatrice glared at her father's retreating back. The problem was, he was just too nice. If he found termites gnawing through the floor, he'd offer them a glass of milk to wash it down.

"Come on then," Beatrice said, sounding anything but gracious.

Amanda and Jason craned their necks and gaped at everything as they followed her into the living room. *They're only here to poke around,* Beatrice thought. To see if the stories about strange goings-on in the Bailey house were true. But she had to give them credit; it took nerve to just show up at the door and invite themselves in. Most of the kids from school wouldn't have had the guts.

Beatrice turned on a lamp and pointed to chairs where they could sit. Instead, Amanda and Jason crowded close together on the sofa. They were looking anxious now, Beatrice noted, and she couldn't hold back a grin. Which seemed to make Amanda even more jittery. She studied Beatrice's amused expression and began to chew on her thumbnail.

Beatrice glanced around the room, trying to see it through their eyes. Everything looked pretty ordinary to her. But then her attention was drawn to the window where three witch balls shimmered in the lamplight. Okay, there were *those*, but witch balls were sold everywhere these days. Mom and Dad even stocked them at the nursery.

Amanda's eyes followed Beatrice's to the globes of green, blue, and ruby red glass. "Those are pretty,"

Amanda said. "Didn't people used to hang them in the window to guard against . . . uh . . . witches?"

Jason glanced sharply at Amanda, who had suddenly gone very pale.

"Is that what people believed?" Beatrice asked sweetly. *Which just goes to show how little mortals know*, she thought. In actual fact, a witch ball in the window was like having a blinking neon sign that read: Witches Welcome Here!

"I'll go help Mom with the snacks," Beatrice added, and left the room. Once out the door, she ducked behind a huge asparagus fern and leaned against the wall to listen. Cayenne brushed past without giving Beatrice so much as a glance, and ambled into the living room.

Beatrice heard Jason whisper, "I don't think this was such a great idea."

"Since when did you start thinking?" Amanda muttered.

Yep, they were getting nervous, all right. Beatrice watched Cayenne wind her way around the legs of an end table, then leap into a chair across from the sofa. She couldn't see Amanda and Jason, but she heard a sudden intake of breath.

"Oh—it's just a cat," Jason said.

"Don't witches use cats as their familiars?"

"Good grief, Amanda, you don't really believe all that mumbo jumbo, do you?"

"I guess not," Amanda said in a small voice.

A moment later, Beatrice saw Jason cross the room to her father's desk. He picked up a book that was bound in black leather. The binding was cracked and faded with age.

"*The Bailiwick Family History*," Jason read. "Whew, it smells like something died—" Then he let out a screech and flung the book into the air. It landed with a thump on the desk.

"What's wrong with you?" Amanda hissed. "They'll *hear* you."

"It's got *bugs* in it!" Jason said in a hoarse whisper. "Huge black beetles!"

Beatrice heard an uneasy laugh. Then Amanda said, "Poor little Jasie, afraid of the big bad bugs."

"It was like they were *guarding* the book."

"Honestly, Jason," Amanda said crossly. "And you accuse *me* of believing in mumbo jumbo."

Beatrice saw Amanda walk over to the desk and pick up the book. "I don't see any bugs."

"Not now—since I scared them all away!"

Amanda giggled. "The bugs weren't the only ones scared."

"And there were cobwebs, too! That book's creepy, Manda."

"*I'll* tell you what's creepy," Amanda said, placing the book on the desk and turning around. "There's something peculiar about that cat. It hasn't taken its eyes off me since it came in here."

From where Beatrice crouched, she could see that Cayenne's eyes were opened wide, giving her the look of a startled owl. And she did seem to be staring directly at Amanda's face.

"This whole place gives me the shivers," Amanda said. "And there's *definitely* something wrong with the parents."

"That's what my dad says, but Mom won't buy plants

from anyone else. Did I tell you the weird advice Mr. Bailey gave her when one of her rosebushes was dying?"

"Uh-uh."

"He said to take three drops of blood from her left foot," Jason said, "and mix it into the soil around the roots of the rosebush—but it had to be done exactly at midnight when the moon was full."

"Surely she didn't do it!"

"Didn't she?" Jason's voice had risen sharply. "And you know what the weirdest part was? It worked! In a few days, that rosebush was sprouting out all over the place."

"Coincidence."

"Maybe . . . but you can't convince my mom of that. She says the Baileys work *magic* with her garden."

"Magic," Amanda murmured. Then she asked suddenly, "Did you notice that Beatrice was barefoot? Olivia Klink's aunt lives next door and she told Olivia's mother that Beatrice and Mrs. Bailey go barefoot all winter."

"In the snow?"

"No, *stupid*, inside the house. But it's still too cold to go barefoot! And look at those strange kids Beatrice hangs out with," Amanda continued, her voice taking on a malicious tone. "Teddy Berry and Cyrus Rascallion and—What's his name? The one that's home schooled?— Ollie something or other. And what about that cat? Olivia's aunt says all Beatrice has to do is stare into its eyes, and the mangy old thing will jump up on her shoulder and sit there like a vulture. It's positively *witchy*!"

"Amanda, let's get out of here."

"We haven't found any evidence."

"Who cares?"

"I do," Amanda said stubbornly. "I want to prove that these people are up to no good."

Suddenly the cat jumped from the table to the piano, and the piano began to play. Ragtime. Beatrice realized at once that Cayenne had hit the switch when she leaped, but Amanda and Jason didn't know it was a player piano. Amanda screamed and Jason yelped, and they were holding onto each other and looking terrified when Beatrice rushed in to turn off the music.

It was about that time that Mrs. Bailey arrived with a tray of goodies. Little cakes made from oats and honey, a bowl of apples, and hot chocolate with cinnamon sticks. Beatrice's mother heard enough disjointed comments to understand what had happened, and she laughed. Mrs. Bailey had a robust laugh. Amanda and Jason stared at her as if she had gone mad.

"Has our wayward cat been tickling the ivories again?" Mrs. Bailey asked. "That must have been disconcerting. Here, dears, sit down and have something to calm your nerves."

Jason looked ready to bolt, but Amanda pushed him into a chair and his knees were too weak to resist. He waited until he saw Mrs. Bailey bite into one of the cakes and Beatrice take a sip of hot chocolate, and then he dug in. It was all delicious. He couldn't remember ever tasting anything as good as those honey cakes.

Mrs. Bailey told them to yell when they needed more food, and left. Beatrice perched on the piano bench and nibbled at the edge of a witch cake—the one thing her mother could cook the regular way without burning it, dissolving it, or turning it to stone.

While Beatrice was considering ways to get rid of these people, Cayenne dropped from the top of the piano onto her shoulder. Amanda saw this and flinched. Cayenne crouched against Beatrice's neck and began to emit her gritty purr. The cat stared with unblinking eyes at Amanda.

All the color had left Amanda's face. She was as white as paper, Beatrice mused. As white as snow. Snow. Beatrice perked up. Of course. *Snow!*

Beatrice began to mumble something under her breath. Jason strained to hear what she was saying. Amanda started to tremble. Beatrice continued to speak in a whisper:

> *Circle of magic, hear my plea.*
> *Blowing winds,*
> *Blinding snow,*
> *These, I ask you, bring to me.*

Beatrice fell silent and turned to look out the window. Amanda looked, too.

"It's snowing," Amanda said in a strangled voice.

"Are you nuts?" Jason's eyes darted to the window. He couldn't miss the thick swirl of snow in the glow of the streetlight. His jaw dropped.

"The wind's picked up, too," Beatrice said. As if on cue, a gust howled around the corner of the house, and snow blew down the chimney into the fireplace.

Amanda gave a startled whimper.

"It seems to be getting worse," Beatrice said, sounding concerned. "I hope you won't have trouble going home."

"But it's only October!" Jason exclaimed.

"We've had snow in October before," Beatrice said.

"This isn't just snow—it's a blizzard!"

"It was sixty degrees today," Amanda said tonelessly. "The sky was perfectly clear."

Amanda looked at Beatrice. She looked at the cat crouched on Beatrice's shoulder. And then she was on her feet and pulling Jason to his.

Beatrice followed them to the front porch. Amanda and Jason hurried down the steps—and sank into snow up to their knees.

"Be careful walking home!" Beatrice called out pleasantly. She resisted the urge to laugh as she watched them lurch and slide toward the street.

Amanda looked back over her shoulder, and Beatrice could see the fury in her eyes. *Uh-oh*, Beatrice thought as she went back inside and closed the door. She would probably end up paying dearly for this little trick. But whatever the price, it had been worth it. Beatrice was still grinning when she carried the snack tray to the kitchen.

She was having another cup of hot chocolate with her mother when the back door swung open and a blast of freezing air filled the room. Mr. Bailey stomped in and slammed the door shut. He was covered with snow, as was the huge potted plant he set down in the middle of the floor.

Beatrice and Mrs. Bailey stared at him.

Mr. Bailey's eyebrows came together in a frown. "This was your doing, I take it," he said to Beatrice.

She knew better than to deny it. Her talents were few, but one thing she could do astonishingly well was control the weather. "Consistently and brilliantly," her father had once exulted to her mother. Beatrice could create a blizzard, a hurricane—any weather condition whatsoever—by simply reciting a weather spell. None of that twitching her nose or waving a wand like the made-up witches on TV. It was all in the recitation.

"Sorry," Beatrice said, and started to explain how hard it was to endure prying classmates like Amanda and Jason.

"Never mind. You have to practice your magic," Mr. Bailey said in a resigned voice. "Just help me bring in the rest of these plants. And next time, give me some warning, would you, please?"

That night, when she was getting ready for bed, Beatrice tried to turn back the covers using magic. She recited a perfectly serviceable spell that she had found in *Good Housekeeping for Witches*, but nothing happened. She tried again, and not a sheet or blanket stirred. Beatrice sighed and folded back the covers the regular way.

Mrs. Bailey stopped by Beatrice's room on her way to bed. Beatrice was sitting up with a book open, but she wasn't reading.

"'Night, darling," Mrs. Bailey said. "Don't stay up too late."

"Mom," Beatrice said, "have we ever had a powerful witch in the family? Or were they all like us?"

"What do you mean, '*like us*'?"

"You know, inept."

Mrs. Bailey blinked, clearly taken aback by her daughter's choice of words. "I wouldn't say we're inept," she said carefully, and came to sit on the edge of Beatrice's bed. "We're *Reform*. We don't rely on magic as much as Traditional witches do, so we aren't as—"

"Good?" Beatrice prompted.

"No."

"Talented?"

Mrs. Bailey shook her head. "Reform witches aren't as *experienced* as Traditional witches. Living among mortals, we have to use our magic discreetly, while Traditionals living in the Witches' Sphere can practice The Craft openly. So their powers are more—developed."

"Were we always Reform?"

"Not always. My great-grandmother was Traditional."

This caught Beatrice's interest. "Did she live in a castle?"

"Not even Traditional witches have been able to afford castles for a while. But she had the next best thing—a big, drafty old house situated at a crossroads."

Beatrice wasn't impressed. She herself lived in a big, drafty old house. It wasn't at a crossroads, but how much difference could that make?

"So why did we go Reform?"

Mrs. Bailey shrugged. "I don't really know. But I imagine that someone in the family got tired of the old ways. You know—stirring up potions from eye of newt and toe of frog, and wearing the same dusty robes and pointed hats every day. So they probably said to themselves, 'Why not go Reform and benefit from mortal inventions and progress?'"

"I can do without the frogs and the dusty robes," Beatrice said thoughtfully, "but I wouldn't mind feeling more competent. Traditional witch kids go to witch academies, don't they? I'll bet they learn to cast spells in kindergarten."

Mrs. Bailey was looking concerned. "Aren't you happy being mainstreamed, sweetheart? I really don't think you'd like it at the witch academy. Why, those poor children study magic all day and all night, and don't even get summers off. Besides," she added firmly, having convinced herself that she knew what was best for Beatrice, "you have two hours a week with your witch tutor. That's enough time to learn all the magic you'll ever need."

Beatrice nodded and produced a smile that was meant to be reassuring. She didn't have the heart to tell her mother that the witch tutor had announced to the whole class that Beatrice's powers were next to useless. He had even suggested—with cruel enjoyment, it had seemed to Beatrice—that she limit her magic to parlor games, since no one took weather control seriously anymore.

"Is everything all right at school?" Mrs. Bailey probed. "Are you having any problems?"

"Everything's fine," Beatrice said quickly. "It's just— sometimes I wish I knew more about casting spells and stuff like that."

Mrs. Bailey smiled and brushed Beatrice's bangs out of her face. "You know, you don't have to cast spells to have magic in your life."

Beatrice rolled her eyes. Her mother was always coming up with something sappy like that.

"'Night, Mom."

Beatrice slid down under the covers. She fell asleep almost as soon as Mrs. Bailey turned out the light. And she had that dream again, the one where she was walking through a field of grass that was too brilliantly green to be real. The light around her was golden, as if sunbeams had been ground to a fine dust and then flung into the air. She could hear the sound of a flute and sweet high voices singing words in a language she didn't understand. Somehow, Beatrice knew that this magical place really did exist outside her dreams. It was just waiting—somewhere—for her to find it.

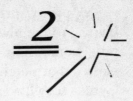

The Fiendish
Four

"**S**tudents in the primary class, continue to work on your witches' alphabet," Mr. Belcher boomed. "Or *Runes of Theban Script*, to use the scholarly term. Write each rune ten times. And remember, fine penmanship is the sign of a cultivated witch."

Mr. Belcher stood behind a massive desk that had carvings of gargoyles across the front and serpents entwined around the legs. The desk took up most of the floor space in the cramped study, leaving no room for student seating. The thirteen fledgling witches in District Eight were required to perch on window ledges and stacks of ancient spell books.

"Intermediates, your assignments are floating on the ceiling," Mr. Belcher added.

And sure enough, when Beatrice looked up, she saw hazy, blue gray script wafting above her head like a thread of smoke.

"I'll read, you write," said a boy at her elbow. He was small and dark, with a wide mouth that smiled easily and vivid blue eyes.

A pretty girl with short brown curls said, "No way, Cyrus. You're always impatient to leave and end up skipping something important." She pushed up wire-rim glasses that perched on the end of her nose and, ignoring Cyrus's scowl, added, "*I'll* read the assignments."

Pen poised, Beatrice said, "Okay, Teddy, shoot."

"Read Chapter 3 for Witch History, Chapter 2 for Seasons of Magic, and Chapters 3 and 4 for Divination," Teddy read.

"Chapter 4 for Divination is optional," Cyrus cut in.

Teddy frowned. "Optional or not, since Mr. Belcher included it, we should read it."

"If we have time. But since it's *optional*," Cyrus said stubbornly, "it doesn't have the same relative importance as the *required* readings, now does it?"

"Be quiet, you two," Beatrice said crossly. She was already unhappy about the long list of assignments, which made Cyrus and Teddy's incessant arguing all the more irritating. "I'll read *and* write."

"It's not fair for you to have to do both," Teddy said, appearing contrite. "Cyrus, why don't you finish reading?"

Cyrus's mouth stretched into a good-natured grin, and he began to rattle off the rest of the assignments. "Study Chapter 2 for a quiz in Witch Etiquette. Gather ten herbs and identify their magical properties for Herbs and Their Uses."

"How much more?" Beatrice mumbled.

She had spoken too softly for Mr. Belcher to have heard her, but he chose that moment to say, "There's one more assignment for you intermediates that I forgot to write down. And that is to create a spell to banish pesky elves from the garden."

The witch tutor was smiling—*sadistically*, Beatrice thought—his little black eyes flitting from face to face as if he wanted to savor the frustration he saw in each. Eugenius Belcher was tall and gnarly, with shoulders that hunched forward and a chest that curved in like the letter C. He was wearing a bright yellow polo shirt and red plaid walking shorts, and he could have passed easily for a mortal except for the green leather shoes with long, pointy toes that he kept tripping over.

"Elves in the garden," Beatrice muttered, and began to shove books into her backpack. She wasn't convinced that elves even existed outside of fairy tales, so how were they supposed to banish something that was probably just a figment of Belcher's overactive imagination? That would be just like him, to give them an impossible assignment.

Mr. Belcher, who had been known to demonstrate his name rudely and often, was still surveying them with a faintly sinister expression. Then his eyes came to rest on Cyrus. "Mr. Rascallion," the witch tutor said coldly, and burped.

Cyrus looked up warily. Mr. Belcher seemed to take special pleasure in tormenting him. The witch tutor enjoyed baiting Beatrice and Teddy, too, of course—to be honest, there was no one Mr. Belcher *didn't* persecute from time to time—but everyone knew that he took a singular delight in humiliating Cyrus.

The class had grown quiet, waiting to see what would happen next.

"Mr. Rascallion, I expect you might have more difficulty than usual with the elf-banishing spell," the witch tutor said, "inasmuch as I suspect that there's a bit of the elf or the brownie in your own family tree."

Someone in the back giggled. Scholastica Ticklepleaser was Beatrice's guess. No one worked harder than Scholastica at playing up to the tutor, which included sniggering regularly at his verbal attacks on her classmates.

"Or perhaps I should say family *bush*," Mr. Belcher said with a particularly nasty sneer. "The Rascallions are all *small*, you see," he explained to the rest of the class.

More giggles. Beatrice glared at the tutor. He ignored her.

"Don't you agree, class, that there's something decidedly *elfin* about Mr. Rascallion? Small. Dark. *Sprightly*," he said wickedly.

This time, no one giggled, but Mr. Belcher was so wrapped up in his own witticisms that he didn't seem to notice. "*Pixieish!*" the witch tutor screeched. To a silent room. Students had begun to look uneasy and were drifting toward the door.

Beatrice pulled the straps of her backpack over her shoulders and blew her bangs out of her eyes. "Come on," she said to Cyrus and Teddy. "Let's get out of here."

"*Gnomish! Fairylike!*"

Mr. Belcher's shrieks and chortles followed them down a hallway that was shrouded in cobwebs and littered with mouse droppings. They stepped out into the crisp, clean air, leaving behind the smells of dust and sulfur—and the bluster and howls of their witch tutor. No one spoke until they were a block away from Mr. Belcher's house.

"He had to give us all this work before Fall Break,"

Beatrice complained. "I was hoping we'd have a week off with no homework."

"*He* doesn't care about the mortal school calendar," Cyrus said. "Sometimes I wish—"

"What?" Teddy said. "What do you wish?"

"That I could master a spell to send Belcher flying beyond the Witches' Sphere!" Cyrus managed a lopsided grin. "Right. Like I'm ever going to master any spell at all."

"There's your shrinking spell," Beatrice pointed out. "That's a great one."

"Yeah—I can do *one* spell," Cyrus said fiercely. "What kind of witch does that make me?"

"The same kind I am," Beatrice said, smiling.

"And me," Teddy said. "There's only one spell I can cast with any degree of confidence. And Ollie, too. We're all in the same boat."

"So they won't be giving us scholarships to the witch academy," Beatrice said with a shrug. "Who cares?"

"*I* care," Teddy said. She saw the corners of Beatrice's mouth begin to lift again and she clenched her jaw. "Well, I *do*! The only thing I've ever wanted in my whole life is to be a great witch. That includes being rich and famous, of course. But how can I hope to learn anything from Belcher? How can I compete with witches who spend hours and hours every day studying with the finest scholars in the Witches' Sphere?" Teddy's voice had risen an octave and she looked like she might burst into tears. "It's *so unfair*!"

"If it means that much to you," Cyrus said, "apply to one of the academies."

Teddy mumbled something.

"What did you say?" Cyrus asked.

"I *said*, I did apply. To *five* academies." Teddy glared at her feet as she walked. "None of them accepted me."

"It's their loss," Beatrice said loyally.

Teddy shot her an irritated look. "I know you're trying to help, but you're only making it worse."

"Well, pardon me," Beatrice muttered. Then, feeling sorry for Teddy, she added, "Those academies are just being snobbish. Parents only send their kids there so they won't have to associate with mortals."

"Or with Everyday witches," Teddy said. "And it works. They sure didn't want me."

"If I applied, they wouldn't accept me, either," Beatrice said, "but you don't see me crying about it."

Teddy said with great dignity, "First of all, Beatrice, you haven't applied, so you don't know that they wouldn't accept you. And second, you haven't been classified as an Everyday witch."

"She's right," Cyrus said. "Teddy and Ollie and I have. We *know* we're Everyday."

"I know I'm Everyday, too," Beatrice said.

"No," Teddy said firmly. "You won't know until the Witches' Executive Committee tells you how you've been classified. You won't know until you're twelve."

"Okay, okay," Beatrice said, "then I'll know for sure in four days. But you don't really expect the committee to say, 'Beatrice Bailey, you have an extraordinary talent for magic. It's just been hidden all these years. Your witch tutor was wrong. *Everyone* was wrong. We're going to classify you as a Classical witch and send you to the best witch academy in the Witches' Sphere. And someday you'll be the greatest witch of all time and have your picture on a cereal box.'"

Beatrice stopped to catch her breath and to enjoy watching Teddy and Cyrus laugh at her response. It was rewarding to see the beginning of a grin on Cyrus's face, but Teddy looked as somber as ever. And on top of that, her face had turned bright red. This was when Beatrice realized that she had just voiced Teddy's most longed-for wish and made a joke of it.

"Uh—It *would* be terrific," Beatrice said hastily, "to be able to cast all kinds of spells. But magic should be fun. Traditionals take it way too seriously. And Traditionals who make it to Classical—well, I'll bet *they* don't have any fun at all. Teddy, all this aspiring to be a *great witch* just takes the joy out of everything!"

No one spoke for a moment. Then Teddy said in a pained voice, "Does that mean I shouldn't have any dreams at all?"

"No, of course it doesn't," Beatrice said.

"Hold on to your dreams," Cyrus advised gravely.

"I might do better in witch class if Belcher didn't make me so nervous." Teddy sighed. "I wish I could trade places with Ollie. Wouldn't it be fantastic to come from an old, revered witch family and have parents and grandparents to teach you? Then you wouldn't need a jerk like Belcher."

"Except that hasn't gone without a snag, either," Cyrus pointed out.

"What do you mean?"

Cyrus looked uncomfortable. "You know," he said reluctantly. "Ollie's had twelve years of in-house training, and he was classified Everyday, too."

"Oh. Yeah."

"What does a dumb classification mean, anyhow?" Beatrice demanded.

"A Classical classification means they think you're capable of important magic," Cyrus said unnecessarily, "whereas they don't expect anything but the occasional goof up from Everydays."

"They, they, they," Beatrice grumbled. "Don't you think the Witches' Executive Committee ever makes a mistake?"

"Probably not," Cyrus said.

"Well, I bet they do," Beatrice said. "And Saturday night, when they announce that they've classified me as an Everyday witch, I'm going to tell them that I'll be whatever I want to be. I'll tell them that I don't *care* how they've classified me."

Cyrus's eyebrows shot up. "Will you really, Beatrice?"

"Of course, she won't," Teddy said.

"I *might*," Beatrice replied, and was pleased to see that she had finally made Teddy smile.

They were approaching Beatrice's house. It was big and old and white, like most of the other houses on the street, but it was the only one in the neighborhood with lime green shutters. If Mrs. Bailey had had her way, she would have painted the whole house lime green, with a turquoise porch and purple steps and bright pink trim. But conservative decorating was one of the concessions Reforms had to make. Except for the shutters, the house looked pretty ordinary. There were tons of leaves that needed to be raked, a pumpkin patch out back, and an untidy herb garden beside the kitchen door.

24

Cayenne was perched on the newel post in the front hall, waiting for her mistress. Teddy watched enviously as Beatrice picked up the cat and they greeted each other with pats and purrs.

"I wish I could have a cat," Teddy said for the hundredth time.

"But with your little brother's allergies—" Cyrus began.

"I know, I know," Teddy interrupted impatiently. "I just said, I wish. Traditional witches always have a familiar to help with their magic and to do their bidding."

Beatrice smiled as she scratched a blissful Cayenne under the chin. "Well, in my case, there isn't much magic to help with."

"And Cayenne isn't exactly the biddable type," Cyrus finished.

Beatrice gave him a look that suggested she might be insulted on her cat's behalf. Then she called out, "Mom, I'm home."

There was no answer.

"That's funny," Beatrice remarked. "She said she was coming home early to cook."

"To cook?" Teddy echoed. Not good, her expression plainly said.

"Maybe she forgot," Cyrus suggested. "They'll probably bring home burgers."

Beatrice started for the kitchen. "Burgers last night. I'll put my money on Chinese."

They passed through the dining room. Beatrice was surprised to see that the door to the kitchen was closed. She turned the knob and pushed. The door wouldn't open.

She pushed harder, without success.

"There's no lock on this door," Beatrice said. "What could be holding it shut?"

"It must be blocked," Cyrus said.

"With what?" Beatrice wanted to know, and called for her mother again.

The answer came from the dining room as Mrs. Bailey ran up behind them. "Beatrice, thank goodness you're here."

Beatrice took one look at her mother and knew that something wasn't right. Mrs. Bailey's face was flushed and damp, her hair was sticking out in all directions, and she had a dazed expression. She didn't look herself at all.

"Mom, what's wrong?" Beatrice asked. "What's keeping the kitchen door shut?"

Mrs. Bailey sighed. "Bread," she said.

Beatrice and her friends gave Mrs. Bailey a strange look. Then Beatrice leaned her shoulder against the door and shoved. Teddy and Cyrus shoved, too. The door moved a little, but not much. Just enough for them to get a strong whiff of yeast and to allow something to squish out around the edges. Beatrice peered closer. She thought it looked like dough. But that couldn't be right, could it? She turned back to her mother.

"Mom, you didn't—"

"I did!" Mrs. Bailey watched in horror as more raw dough squeezed through the crack around the door. "I cast a little spell to make the bread rise, and then left for just a minute. When I came back, the dough had oozed out of the oven and across the kitchen floor. It kept coming and coming," Mrs. Bailey said, sounding on the verge of hysteria, "and rising and rising. Until it pushed me out the door and into the yard!"

Cyrus started laughing.

"It isn't funny," Mrs. Bailey cried. "What can we do to stop it?"

"Isn't there a counterspell?" Beatrice asked her mother.

"Oh, dear, if there is, I don't know it."

"The spell is probably self-limiting," Teddy said. "At some point, the dough should stop rising on its own."

And so it did. But not until dough had filled every square inch of the Baileys' kitchen.

They were cleaning up when Ollie arrived. Most of the dough had already been carried out in pans and baskets to the backyard. Beatrice wondered what the neighbors would think when they looked out their windows and saw that the Baileys' lawn had become a giant pizza crust.

"Yipes! What happened here?" Ollie took a step into the kitchen, then stopped. Bits of dough still clung to countertops, appliances—and even the ceiling, Beatrice realized, as a big glob fell from the light fixture and splattered on Ollie's head.

He took it with good grace, as he did most things. Ollie Tibbs might not be a brilliant witch, but he was, under nearly any set of circumstances, a gentleman. He reached up without comment and scooped most of the goo out of his hair.

"Here," Beatrice said, holding out a bucket.

"A spell gone awry?"

Beatrice nodded.

Ollie didn't ask anymore, which just goes to show how much of a gentleman he really was. He tied on an apron and pitched in to help with the cleanup.

Ollie was nearly as skinny as Beatrice, and half a head

taller, with green eyes and hair the color of custard pie. Beatrice thought he was the most handsome boy she had ever seen. She liked him a lot. Maybe she even had a bit of a crush on him, but she didn't want to think about that yet. Beatrice wasn't ready for a change in their old, familiar relationship.

The four of them—Beatrice, Teddy, Ollie, and Cyrus —had always been best friends. Because of their tendency to get into mischief whenever they were together, and their fierce defense of each other from outside attack, Mr. Bailey had dubbed them "the fiendish four" when they were still in nursery school. Despite their very different personalities, the friends had become even closer as they grew older. Certainly, their unique status in a town inhabited almost solely by mortals had fostered a special devotion among the four.

After Ollie had been helping clean the kitchen for a few minutes, watching everyone bump into each other as they ran to dump a bucket or pot or basket of dough into the yard, he said, "I think I know a faster way."

They all stopped to listen because Ollie was good at problem solving.

"Why don't we form a chain?" he suggested. "The first person fills a container, then passes it down the line until the last person gets it and dumps it into the yard."

"Great idea!" they exclaimed. "Why didn't we think of that before?"

Using Ollie's method, they finished cleaning the kitchen before Mr. Bailey came home from the nursery. And Beatrice had been right—he brought enough Chinese food for everyone.

"I'd better be going home," Teddy said when they had finished off the last of the moo goo gai pan.

Cyrus and Ollie remarked that they should leave, too, but continued to nibble on egg rolls and fried wonton.

"Don't forget Beatrice's birthday party," Mrs. Bailey said. "It's Saturday night."

"Mom, you've only reminded them thirty-seven times," Beatrice said. "How embarrassing."

Mrs. Bailey smiled. "Your friends understand, sweetie. They have annoying parents of their own."

"Beatrice, your mother found a spell for a birthday cake that replenishes itself after it's been eaten," Mr. Bailey said as he gathered up the trash.

"Oh?" Beatrice glanced at her mother, who ducked her head and busied herself with wiping fried rice off the table.

"She hasn't used her magic in so long, I thought she might as well give it a shot," Mr. Bailey continued. "I mean, how much damage can a cake spell do?"

Beatrice exchanged a look with Ollie. Teddy started to giggle—then stopped when Mrs. Bailey cleared her throat and frowned.

"I've found a great band," Mr. Bailey went on as he headed out the door with the trash. "You're going to love it, Beatrice."

Beatrice waited until her father had left and closed the door behind him. Then she said, "Mom, he didn't hire those ghouls from last year, did he? They were hopeless."

"Yeah," Teddy said, "the only music they knew were funeral dirges."

"I think this is a different band," Mrs. Bailey said.

"You *think*?"

"Anyway," her mother added, "the music isn't the most important part of the celebration."

"Not compared to the food and the presents," Cyrus agreed.

"You'll be twelve this year," Mrs. Bailey said to Beatrice, sounding proud, excited, and sad all at the same time.

"Right. It's time for the Witches' Executive Committee to seal your doom." Teddy didn't look like she was kidding.

"I know it made *my* whole year," Ollie said with a grin.

"It's good that you can joke about it," Teddy said gently. They all knew that Ollie's father and mother and grandparents and uncles and aunts—and everyone else in the family—had been devastated when they heard Ollie's classification. There hadn't been an Everyday witch in the Tibbs family in over a hundred years.

"What's the big deal, anyhow?" Beatrice asked, trying for a casual tone to mask her anxiety. She really wasn't looking forward to facing the Witches' Executive Committee. "Once and for all, there's *nothing wrong with being an Everyday witch.*"

Mr. Bailey came back inside, shivering in his shirt-sleeves. "A hot cup of All-Hallows tea would be good right now," he said.

"Can everyone stay?" Mrs. Bailey asked. "I'll have it brewed in a shake."

Teddy and Cyrus replied that their parents expected them home. But Ollie said, "Let me help, Mrs. Bailey."

Dozens of glass jars filled with powders and crushed leaves lined the kitchen wall above the stove. From among the bottles labeled *Wolfsbane* and *Madwort* and *Thornapple*, Beatrice's mother gathered up the ingredients for tea. While she measured out the orris root powder and dried violet petals, Ollie filled a pot with water and chanted:

Heat of flame, heat of fire,
Give to me my one desire.
Boil this water, bubbling free,
As my will, so mote it be!

The pot of water began to boil.

"Thanks, Ollie," Mrs. Bailey said, and dropped in the tea leaves.

At the Stroke
of Midnight

Beatrice had always looked forward to birthdays. She had certainly never dreaded one before. But as her twelfth birthday approached, her uneasiness grew. Now that she faced being told formally—and publicly—that she was nothing special, Beatrice was beginning to understand why classification as an Everyday witch bothered Teddy and Ollie so much. (And perhaps Cyrus as well, but he didn't seem to dwell on it.) The classification was so—*final*. Even humiliating, Beatrice supposed, if you were Teddy and wanted nothing more than to be the greatest witch in the world. Or Ollie, with a zillion relatives hanging their heads and wailing, "The *shame* of it!"

Teddy came over on Saturday morning to help Beatrice decorate for the party.

"First, you have to see my dress," Beatrice said.

They raced upstairs to Beatrice's room, ducking as they passed through the doorway to miss a large spiderweb and the spider that was weaving it.

When Teddy saw the pale red dress hanging on the closet door, she said softly, "Oh, Beatrice, it's *beauuuu-tiful.* I can't believe your mother made this."

Beatrice beamed. Her mother's ability with a sewing machine was nothing short of magical, but Beatrice thought she had outdone herself this time.

Teddy ran her fingers lightly over the velvet ribbon and porcelain beads that Mrs. Bailey had sewn across the bodice. The long, full skirt swayed and whispered under her hand.

"It's almost the same shade as your hair," Teddy said. "You're going to be gorgeous."

"Right." Beatrice looked embarrassed, but pleased. "Does that mean you've mastered the Make-Beatrice-Gorgeous spell?"

They went downstairs and Beatrice brought out bags filled with rolls of crepe-paper streamers and packages of balloons.

"We're decorating like mortals," she said apologetically. "Shows no imagination whatsoever."

As Beatrice began to unwind a roll of yellow crepe paper, Cayenne appeared out of nowhere and grabbed the end of the streamer. The cat leaped and spun and twirled until she was wrapped up like a fat yellow mummy.

With Cayenne's help, it took a while to decorate. Teddy was hanging the last cluster of balloons when Mr. Bailey came in carrying a large box.

"I ordered these weeks ago," he said, sounding excited. "I was beginning to think they wouldn't get here in time."

Beatrice and Teddy watched him open the box, remove lots of bubble wrap, and then scoop out handfuls of small glass orbs that looked like clear marbles.

"What are they?" Beatrice asked.

"You'll see," her father said. "Now, where's that package of magic dust? Oh, good, here it is. Beatrice, you and Teddy pile all the globes together—that's right—and I'll sprinkle the dust on them."

Mr. Bailey ripped open an envelope and poured out a glistening powder into his palm. "Tickles a little!" he said with a chuckle, and began to sprinkle the powder over the globes. When the magic dust touched them, they rose into the air, and then they began to glow.

"They're lights!" Beatrice exclaimed.

"*Magic* lights," Mr. Bailey said, still sprinkling the dust and grinning as more balls floated upward. "Aren't they something?"

"They're wonderful."

"And so is your magic," Teddy said. "You pulled it off without a hitch, Mr. Bailey."

"Well—it's not exactly *my* magic," he admitted. "It's packaged magic. From the Real Good Magic Company."

"I love it," Beatrice said. "Thanks, Dad. The lights add just the right touch."

Mr. Bailey was grinning again. "They're supposed to float and glow for twenty-four hours without more dust."

"Let's pull the shades and see how they look in the dark," Beatrice said.

With the shades lowered, the magic lights resembled fireflies twinkling across the ceiling.

"Great effect," Teddy said.

When Mr. Bailey left to go back to the nursery, Beatrice and Teddy started to tidy up the room. Teddy was raising one of the shades when she suddenly jumped back and gave a startled squeak.

"What's wrong?" Beatrice asked her.

"I saw a face. In that bush," Teddy said, pointing out the window. "It disappeared when it saw me looking."

"Chester Sidebottom."

"What?"

"A nosy little boy from across the street. He's always spying on us. Once he told his parents that my father was flying around our living room." Beatrice smiled. "It was when Dad tried using magic to paint the walls. He cast a spell to help him reach the high spots, but it backfired—made him shoot across the room like a comet."

"So what did Chester's parents do?"

"Grounded him for making up stories about the neighbors." Beatrice laughed, then became serious again. "Or maybe you saw one of the kids from school. They're dying to prove the Baileys aren't normal."

Teddy made a face. "As if you'd *want* to be," she said. "Why don't I find out if it's dear little Chester or not? Come look out the window with me."

Beatrice went to the window, and Teddy began to chant:

> *Candle, bell, and willow tree,*
> *Who does stalk and spy on me?*
> *With your magic, with your charm,*
> *Show us who would do us harm.*

Suddenly, the bushes outside the window sprang apart. Amanda Bugg was crouched behind them, unaware that her cover had been blown.

"*Her*," Teddy said. "Doesn't she know when to quit?"

"Maybe I can help her learn," Beatrice said softly, and began to mutter under her breath.

There was a sudden rumble of thunder. Lightning flashed. Rain poured. Amanda leaped up and started to run. She sank into mud up to her ankles and her shoes were sucked off her feet. The girl sprinted toward the street, barefoot, muddy, and soaked to the skin, with thunder crashing and lightning crackling all around her.

A block away, the sun was shining.

Family and friends started arriving at the Bailey house around eight that evening. Before long, there were fifty witches eating, drinking, talking, laughing, and trying to dance to the music of Fire & Brimstone. That was the name of the band Mr. Bailey had hired.

"What do you think?" Beatrice asked Ollie. They were watching three middle-aged male witches in bell bottoms and tie-dyed T-shirts play seventies music that no one had cared for even back then.

"Well, it's *livelier* than last year's band," Ollie said.

Just then Teddy walked up. "This music. How do we dance to it?" She was wearing a long black dress and a black silk hat with a pointed crown that flopped stylishly to one side.

"If I didn't know better, I'd swear you were Traditional," Beatrice said admiringly.

Teddy looked pleased. "Thanks, old friend. And you're just as dazzling as I knew you would be. Don't you agree, Ollie?"

"Absolutely," Ollie said, smiling. He had been watching Beatrice all evening, much to her confusion and delight.

"Only one more week till Fall Break," Teddy said.

"What are you two going to do with your time off?" Ollie asked.

"I'm planning to try on every outfit at the mall." Teddy flashed Beatrice a grin. "And hang out here, if I'm invited."

"You're *always* invited," Beatrice said. "You both are," she added, without looking at Ollie, but she could see the glint of devilment in Teddy's eyes. "And Cyrus, too, of course," she went on hurriedly. "As for Fall Break, I'm going to sleep till noon and spend my afternoons designing a smashing costume for the Tibbses' annual Halloween gala."

"That's right," Teddy said. "I'll have to work on my costume, too. I can't go to the most sensational party of the year in just any old rag."

"Your parents do give the greatest parties," Beatrice said to Ollie.

"They're the best!" Teddy declared, then looked hastily at Beatrice. "Not better than this party, of course. This is *fantastic*."

Beatrice gave her a get-serious look, and said, "Uh-huh. Especially the music."

At midnight, Beatrice was dancing with Cyrus. The clock in the hall sounded the first of twenty-four strikes. Mr. and Mrs. Bailey made their way through the crowd to Beatrice and hugged her.

"It's officially your birthday," Mr. Bailey said.

"Happy birthday, sweetheart," Mrs. Bailey added.

"Thanks for the terrific party," Beatrice was saying, when she noticed a large ball of light coming through the doorway from the hall. Startled guests stepped back to give it space. Then suddenly the ball exploded, and the room was filled with a shower of falling stars and ribbons of fire.

There were gasps and screams. Dust from the explosion spread quickly. People began to cough. Beatrice picked up on bits of conversation around her.

"Of course—she's twelve."

"—from the Witches' Institute—"

"—haven't been to a classification in ages. What fun."

Sure, Beatrice thought. *Fun for them. They weren't going to be told in front of everyone that they were ordinary, run-of-the-mill, garden-variety* Everyday *witches.*

"It will be fine," Mrs. Bailey whispered into Beatrice's ear.

Her mother was right, Beatrice thought. She knew what to expect, so it wouldn't come as a shock. And she owed it to her friends to show them that a dumb classification meant nothing. Nothing at all.

Beatrice took a deep breath. Then she blew her bangs out of her eyes and started toward the doorway . . .

. . . where thirteen witches waited for her.

The Witch of Bailiwick

All thirteen were Traditional witches. They wore flowing robes in jewel-tone colors: berry red, jade green, saffron yellow, mandarin orange, sapphire blue, and royal purple. The witches also wore silk hats that matched their robes and the points flopped to the side as Teddy's did. *That girl has always had a sense of style*, Beatrice thought.

One of the thirteen wore black. This witch stepped forward and raised his arms dramatically. The sleeves of his robes fell back and Beatrice could see that they were lined with gold silk. The man had once been tall, but now he was stooped with age. His gaunt face was framed with untidy white hair, and he had bushy white brows over ice blue eyes.

"I am Dr. Thaddeus Thigpin, Director of the Witches' Institute," he said to Beatrice in a surprisingly powerful voice. "In case your Reform parents haven't advised you of this, the Witches' Institute is the governing body for all witches, Traditional and Reform."

"Of course they've told me," Beatrice said, resenting the implied insult. But there was no point in making this meeting more unpleasant than it had to be, she decided, so she took a deep breath and smiled. "I'm Beatrice Bailey. I expect you're here to give me my class—"

"Bailey? *Bailey?*" Dr. Thigpin was rifling through papers on a clipboard. "I don't see *anything* about a Bailey. It's Beatrice *Bailiwick* we've come to see."

Mr. Bailey pushed through the crowd that had gathered to watch and came to stand beside his daughter. He looked flustered.

"That was our family name originally," he said, and cleared his throat. "Bailiwick, that is. Some relation changed it years ago—when they decided to . . . uh . . . go Reform. Bailiwick is more of a *traditional* name, you see. So as they modernized their lives, they updated the name, as well. To Bailey." He glanced at Beatrice, then looked back at Dr. Thigpin. "I hope you don't hold this against my daughter. It just never seemed all that important."

Dr. Thigpin was watching him with those pale cold eyes. "Of course not," he said in a quiet voice. "Why should one's family name be considered important? One's family *history*. All you Reforms are just alike. Modernize, modernize. Forget tradition and honor and—"

"Thaddeus."

"—everything glorious in our past—"

"Thaddeus!" A thirty-something witch with auburn hair spilling over the shoulders of her sapphire blue robes jerked on his sleeve. "This isn't the time or the place," she said out of the corner of her mouth. "We've obviously found the right witch, so let's get on with it, shall we?"

Dr. Thigpin pulled himself up as tall as his rounded shoulders would allow and straightened his robes. "Very well, Aura," he said.

"Thank you, Thaddeus," she responded graciously, and glanced at Beatrice before looking around the room. Beatrice wasn't positive, but she thought the woman had winked at her.

"These twelve witches and I comprise the Executive Committee of the Witches' Institute," Dr. Thigpin said to Beatrice. "I am the Institute director and each of these witches is director of one of the Institute's functions. Dr. Aura Featherstone," he said, nodding toward the auburn-haired witch, "is Director of Witch Classification. Dr. Featherstone is the one who finalizes a classification— that is, Classical witch or Everyday witch—after the full committee has voted on it."

"Every witch is observed until his or her twelfth birthday," Dr. Featherstone said, looking intently at Beatrice. "In most cases, the appropriate classification is apparent by that time."

Just tell me, Beatrice thought, feeling more miserable by the moment. *Tell me I'm Everyday, ordinary, run-of-the-mill—and let us get back to our party.*

Dr. Thigpin was frowning at Beatrice. He seemed about to say something that he would prefer not to say. What he said was, "Sometimes, however, the commit-tee isn't in agreement about a classification. Rarely," he added quickly. "It's a *very* rare occurrence. But it's happened with you." Dr. Thigpin had such a fierce expression that he looked like he might start baying at the moon any moment. "It wasn't perfectly clear to all members of the committee what your classification should be."

What? Beatrice stared at Dr. Thigpin's scowling face. She glanced at Dr. Featherstone, who appeared considerably more pleasant. Beatrice looked around for the other members of the Witches' Executive Committee, and discovered that all but one had apparently lost interest and wandered over to the food table. The one who remained with Dr. Thigpin and Dr. Featherstone was wearing yellow robes and had a cap of brown hair that reminded Beatrice of a toadstool. He smiled kindly at her, and she was so grateful for a friendly gesture that she gave him a glowing smile in return.

"This is Dr. Leopold Meadowmouse, Director of Witch Holidays," Dr. Featherstone said.

"It's a pleasure to meet you, Beatrice," Dr. Meadowmouse said.

"Must we drag this out forever?" Dr. Thigpin demanded. "Tell her, Aura, as I'm feeling a bit peckish. I'm sure I'm not up to it."

"Certainly, Thaddeus," Dr. Featherstone said, and turned back to Beatrice. "In short, my dear, you haven't been classified. We must test you to see if you have the potential to become a Classical witch."

"A test," Beatrice said, feeling dazed. "You mean, a magic test?"

She was pretty sure she heard Dr. Thigpin mutter an oath under his breath. It was becoming exceedingly clear how the director of the Witches' Institute had voted in regard to her classification. He was gazing around the room at the crepe-paper streamers and birthday balloons. She could almost hear him thinking, *How predictably mortal of them.*

"I believe," Dr. Featherstone said, "that it would be more accurate to call it a Noble Quest."

Beatrice had no idea what a Noble Quest was, but she thought it sounded hard.

"I wonder," Dr. Meadowmouse said to Dr. Featherstone, "if we shouldn't begin with the Bailiwick family history."

"A good idea, Leopold."

"Yes, indeed," Dr. Thigpin said scornfully, and walked away to join the other directors at the food table.

"Let me tell her, Aura," Dr. Meadowmouse said eagerly.

Dr. Featherstone nodded, and Dr. Meadowmouse radiated happiness. He turned to Beatrice. "As you heard earlier, your family name is Bailiwick, and you have a famous relative—a very wise and powerful sorcerer called Bromwich of Bailiwick."

Dr. Meadowmouse looked over at *The Bailiwick Family History*, which lay closed on the desk. The book suddenly sailed across the room and landed in his hands. It fell open, and a large black beetle crawled out and proceeded to make its way up his arm. Dr. Meadowmouse didn't appear to notice.

"You should read this history sometime," Dr. Meadowmouse said to Beatrice, and brushed a cobweb from the page. "Fascinating family, the Bailiwicks."

"Yes, Leopold," Dr. Featherstone said impatiently, "but we're focusing on Bromwich just now."

"Oh, of course." Dr. Meadowmouse frowned slightly

and peered down at the open book. "As I've already mentioned, Bromwich was powerful," he said, "and good. He had lived for many years in the kingdom of Bailiwick, where it was always springtime, and where everyone was happy all the time."

"Leopold," Dr, Featherstone interrupted sharply, "this isn't a fairy tale. Don't fill the girl's head with make-believe."

"As you wish," Dr. Meadowmouse said, looking offended. "Well, it *was* always springtime in Bailiwick. Will you concede to that, Aura? And it only rained at night, gentle showers to keep the flowers blooming. And *almost* everyone who lived there was *relatively* happy *most* of the time. Is that better, Aura?"

Dr. Featherstone nodded.

"Good!" Dr. Meadowmouse said curtly. "Oh, yes, I almost forgot—Bromwich had four daughters: Rhona, Innes, Ailsa, and Morven. They were very beautiful—*all right*, Aura! If life were perfect, the daughters would have been beautiful and kind and gifted—you get the idea, Beatrice. But this is real life, so the daughters were fairly attractive, and they were nice most of the time, and their talents were better than average."

Dr. Meadowmouse took a deep breath and wiped his face with a saffron yellow hanky. "*Anyway*, everything was going along fine until about two hundred years ago. That's when another sorcerer arrived in Bailiwick. His name was Dally Rumpe, and he was also very powerful. But unlike Bromwich, Dally Rumpe was evil. He envied Bromwich his beautiful kingdom where every—where *almost* everyone was happy *most* of the time."

Dr. Featherstone frowned. "We should probably hurry this up," she said.

"Then *you* tell it, Aura!"

"All right, I will. Dally Rumpe wanted the kingdom of Bailiwick for himself," Dr. Featherstone told Beatrice, "but he wasn't quite powerful enough to take it away from Bromwich. So when he cast his spell, a terrible thing happened—the kingdom split apart. There was the central piece where Bromwich's castle stood, and four others. An enchanted barricade appeared around each of these five regions, making it impossible for anyone except Dally Rumpe to enter or leave. Dally Rumpe wasn't pleased with the outcome, but it was better than nothing, and he was delighted that Bromwich and the good sorcerer's daughters were now his prisoners.

He locked Bromwich in the dungeons of his own castle, and he sent one of Bromwich's daughters to each of the other four regions. None of them is allowed to leave and their powers are useless as long as they are under Dally Rumpe's curse. He could have had Bromwich and his daughters killed, of course, but Dally Rumpe knew that they would suffer more if they were kept alive as lonely prisoners throughout eternity."

When the Director of Classification didn't go on, Beatrice said, "That's a terrible thing to have happen—and I don't mean to sound unsympathetic—but what does any of this have to do with me?"

Dr. Featherstone looked at Dr. Meadowmouse. "You have the book, Leopold. Doesn't it spell out her role in some detail?"

"Yes," he said, flipping through the pages, "yes, it does.

Ah—here we are. It says that the eldest Bailiwick female in each generation is tasked with trying to break Dally Rumpe's spell. If she succeeds, the kingdom of Bailiwick will be made whole again, Bromwich and his daughters will be freed from their prisons, and their powers will be restored. And you, Beatrice," he said, looking up and smiling at her, "are the eldest—actually, the *only*—female in your generation."

Beatrice was sure that she couldn't have heard correctly. *She*, Beatrice Bailey . . . uh . . . Bailiwick—*whatever*—was supposed to break a spell cast by a powerful sorcerer? Were these witches for real?

"I know this must seem overwhelming," Dr. Featherstone said.

"You might say that," Beatrice replied. She looked at Dr. Meadowmouse. "You said that this Dally Rumpe showed up two hundred years ago?"

"More or less."

"So what has the eldest Bailiwick female been doing for the past two hundred years? If no one else was willing to go after this evil sorcerer—"

"Oh, but they were," Dr. Meadowmouse said, licking his thumb and turning a page. "Just read your history. Several Bailiwick females have attempted to break the spell."

This doesn't sound good, Beatrice thought. "Obviously, they failed," she said.

"Sadly so," Dr. Meadowmouse replied.

Beatrice sighed. She was beginning to feel very tired. This wasn't exactly the birthday she had anticipated. In fact, it was quickly turning into a major disappointment.

"So what makes you think," she said, looking first at Dr. Meadowmouse and then at Dr. Featherstone, "that I can do any better than my ancestors did?"

"We don't know that you can," Dr. Featherstone said briskly. "But you have an obligation to try. A family obligation. So it seemed the perfect test for your MML."

"My what?"

"MML," Dr. Featherstone repeated. "Maximum Magic Level. If you attain a high enough score—which we never reveal, by the way—you will be classified as a Classical witch."

"And if that happens," Dr. Meadowmouse said earnestly, "you'll be trained at one of the witch academies, and then you'll serve two years in the WSC."

"Witches' Service Corps," Dr. Featherstone said, saving Beatrice the trouble of asking. "They help out during natural disasters. Unnatural ones, too, as necessary."

Beatrice didn't know what to say. It sounded like becoming a Classical witch was a lot more complicated than she had ever imagined. And she didn't even care about being a great witch the way Teddy did. She just didn't want to be made to feel like a failure. But how would she feel, Beatrice wondered, if she were dumb enough to agree to this test and then failed at that? Probably a whole lot worse than she felt right now. Assuming she was still able to feel anything at all. Messing around with this Dally Rumpe sounded dangerous.

Beatrice's parents were standing nearby, looking alarmed.

"*Must* I?" Beatrice asked her mother.

"Certainly not! This test is voluntary." Mrs. Bailey

gave Drs. Featherstone and Meadowmouse an incensed look. "You should have told her that up front."

Meanwhile, Dr. Thigpin had rejoined them. "None of us believes that Dally Rumpe can be bested by a young witch of such limited ability—"

"Don't speak for me, Thaddeus," Dr. Featherstone said sharply.

Dr. Thigpin sniffed. "Aura, I ask you, how many witches—*gifted* witches—have tried to break the spell and failed? But be that as it may," he added, and glared at Beatrice, "*you need to try.*"

This was the last thing Beatrice had expected him to say. "But if you're so sure that I'll fail—"

Dr. Thigpin waved his hand impatiently. "Failing, succeeding—that's not the point. Thanks to your Reform upbringing, you know more about mortals than you do about your own kind. It's time you learned about your family. And past time you found out what it is you're made of."

Beatrice was ready to say no. Politely, but firmly. She had already had enough of these people bossing her around and telling her what was good for her. Not to mention quarreling among themselves and looking down their oh, so, Traditional noses at her family and friends.

But then Teddy whispered so that only Beatrice could hear, "I know you don't like any of this, but it *is* a great honor. How many Reform witches get the chance to become Classical?"

Beatrice didn't know. And at that moment, she didn't especially care.

"Whether you agree to the test or not, you have a

responsibility to help Bromwich, don't you?" Teddy went on. "Can you just walk away from that?"

Beatrice grimaced. She didn't want to hear this.

"And if you don't try, you'll always wonder: *Could I have broken the spell? Do I have what it takes to be Classical?*"

Beatrice didn't want to admit it, but Teddy was right. She *would* always wonder. And poor Bromwich, waiting year after year, century after century, for someone to free him and his daughters. Now that she knew about them—and was beginning to feel a kinship—how could she turn her back on them? *But they deserve better*, Beatrice thought. They deserved someone who knew what she was doing!

"I'll help you," Teddy said, and she must have spoken out loud because Dr. Featherstone said, "Excellent. There's no rule that says the tested witch can't be assisted by friends."

Teddy turned to Cyrus and Ollie. "And you'll help, too," she said firmly. "*Won't* you?"

"Sure," Cyrus replied, and his eyes were already gleaming at the prospect of an adventure.

"Of course, I'll help," Ollie said, looking very serious.

Dr. Featherstone appeared pleased. "Well, Thaddeus," she said, "since these three are going to be involved in the test, as well, it's only fair that we reexamine their classifications, don't you think?"

Dr. Thigpin gave her a long-suffering look.

"It's the honorable thing to do," Dr. Featherstone said mildly.

Teddy was holding her breath. Everyone's eyes were fixed on the Institute director.

"Very well," he said grudgingly. "Not that it's likely to make a difference."

"Maybe yes and maybe no," Dr. Featherstone said.

Beatrice was already wondering if it was too late to back out—and wondering, too, how this had even come about since she didn't remember actually agreeing to the test. But one look at Teddy and Cyrus's brilliant smiles —and was there even a hint of excitement in Ollie's thoughtful expression?—and Beatrice realized that she would probably have to see this through.

"Oh, dear," Dr. Featherstone said suddenly. "I forgot to call Peregrine."

"Call him now," Dr. Meadowmouse said. "He won't have missed much."

The auburn-haired witch muttered something under her breath. This time it was a very small ball of light that appeared in front of her, and then it burst apart with a minuscule flash and the unpresuming pop of a cap pistol. A bit of dust, and a small man in mole brown robes materialized.

He was no more than four feet tall, with very large ears protruding through his toast-colored hair and a small mouth that drooped at the corners. Beatrice noticed that he had long narrow feet sticking out from under his robes, and it occurred to her that he looked less like a witch than a leprechaun, if only he had been wearing green.

Dr. Featherstone said, "Beatrice, this is Peregrine, your witch adviser." She paused, and then added, "And you don't know what a witch adviser is, do you?"

Beatrice was forced to admit that she didn't.

"A witch adviser advises," Dr. Meadowmouse said

helpfully, then grew silent and pink faced under Dr. Featherstone's chilly stare.

"Every young witch who is about to be tested—or is classified as Classical—is assigned a witch adviser," Dr. Featherstone said. "It's Peregrine's job to answer any and all questions you may have about your witchly role, and to guide you as best he can—*without* doing the work that you must do for yourself. Do you understand?"

Probably not, Beatrice thought, but her mind was so full of things that she didn't understand, she was certain that any more explanation would just get lost up there.

"Good!" Dr. Featherstone seemed to consider no answer an affirmative one. "And oh, yes, Peregrine will accompany you on your Noble Quest."

It should have been reassuring that the Executive Committee wasn't expecting Beatrice and her friends to set out on their own with no earthly, or unearthly, idea of what they were doing. But then Beatrice looked at Peregrine. He was staring at his long feet, and he had begun to quiver. Whether shy or nervous or scared out of his wits, Peregrine's demeanor didn't inspire great confidence.

"So when will you leave?" Dr. Featherstone asked.

Mrs. Bailey exchanged a distressed look with Mr. Bailey.

"Uh . . . they shouldn't miss school," Mr. Bailey blurted out.

"Yes," Mrs. Bailey agreed quickly. "Perhaps we could delay this until—next summer?"

"Fall Break starts in a week," Teddy pointed out.

Mrs. Bailey looked deflated. "Oh, yes, Fall Break."

Beatrice knew that her parents didn't want her to go. She thought about using that as an excuse. She couldn't worry her mother sick, could she? But she also knew—down deep, no matter how much she resisted the idea—that she had to go. Not because of the honor, or because it was written in *The Bailiwick Family History* that she must. She had to try to break the spell because the decision shouldn't be based on fear. And Beatrice was afraid. In fact, she was terrified! *That* was why she had to accept the Executive Committee's challenge. And it wouldn't hurt, Beatrice realized, if she and her friends could prove once and for all that Reform witches were every bit as good as Traditionals.

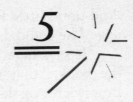

Dally Rumpe's Curse

"**B**ut how do we know what to do?" Beatrice asked. Now that she had accepted the inevitability of her decision, it was time to get practical. "How do we start on this Noble Quest?"

"Why, it's all written in here," Dr. Meadowmouse said, thumping *The Bailiwick Family History* and looking surprised. "You really must sit down and read it, Beatrice. The parts that apply, anyway."

The director of the Witches' Institute was fidgeting. "Aura, you shouldn't be needing me anymore. But feel free to stay as long as you like."

"Thank you for your support, Thaddeus," Dr. Featherstone said.

Dr. Thigpin's response was something just short of a growl. "All those ready to return to the Witches' Sphere, think 'Home again, home again!'" he said loudly. And just like that, eleven of the thirteen committee witches were gone.

Only Drs. Featherstone and Meadowmouse remained.

And timid little Peregrine, of course, who looked as if he *wished* he could disappear.

"It says here," Dr. Meadowmouse said as he studied the book, "that the central region of Bailiwick where Bromwich's castle stands, and where he is imprisoned by Dally Rumpe, has remained much the same. But the other four regions—" He shook his head. "Oh, this is bad, very bad, indeed."

"Tell us, Leopold," Dr. Featherstone said.

"Well, you know, Aura, and—" he turned to look at Beatrice, "perhaps you know as well—that since ancient times, the Wise Ones have recognized that four basic elements are needed to sustain life."

Beatrice looked blank. Dr. Featherstone sighed and said, "Earth, fire, water, and air."

"But when Dally Rumpe split the kingdom with his spell," Dr. Meadowmouse went on, "he upset the delicate balance of the elements, so that one element became dominant in each of the four regions where Bromwich's daughters are imprisoned."

"Oh, that *is* bad," Dr. Featherstone said. "What was the result?"

"Each region has become a land of extremes." Dr. Meadowmouse looked back at the book and ran his finger down the page as he read: "The northern region is called Winter Wood, and its dominant element is air. Winter Wood is horribly cold and buried year-round in snow and ice. Crops won't grow, and people and animals are always living on the edge of starvation."

"Dreadful," Dr. Featherstone murmured.

"There's more," Dr. Meadowmouse said. "Surrounding

the whole of this icy region is an enchanted hedge of thorns that grows so thick and strong neither ax nor magic has been able to penetrate it. The hedge is so tall, it disappears into the clouds, and anyone foolish enough to try to fly over it will be hopelessly lost in the atmosphere and will never be heard from again."

"It's worse than I expected," Dr. Featherstone said. "Is there more?"

"Just the dragon."

Dr. Featherstone nodded. "Of course there would be a dragon."

"An enormous fire-breathing one," Dr. Meadowmouse said. "It guards Bromwich's daughter Rhona."

"Um—I don't know about this," Beatrice said. "I hadn't counted on a dragon."

Ollie nodded his hasty agreement. Even Teddy and Cyrus appeared subdued.

"It says that Winter Wood is the first region the Bailiwick witch must enter," Dr. Meadowmouse said. "Once the spell is broken there, she can move on to the region in the south."

"Tell us about the south," Dr. Featherstone said.

"The dominant element there is earth. This part of the kingdom is very hot and humid, making the people lethargic and lazy. The region is called Werewolf Close."

"Don't tell me," Dr. Featherstone said. "It's guarded by werewolves."

"Exactly right. And the werewolves are hidden in a ring of enchanted fog that blinds and disorients anyone who enters it. The fog is three miles wide and encircles the entire area."

"And the next region?" Dr. Featherstone asked.

"That's the east. The dominant element is water. In fact," Dr. Meadowmouse said, not looking up from the book, "most of the region *consists* of water, with a few small islands sprinkled about. The islands are often flooded by sea surges that drown the crops, as well as the people. The region is called Sea-Dragon Bay, and the water is alive with every type of vicious sea monster that has ever been born, hatched, or imagined."

"Delightful," Beatrice murmured.

"And the fourth region?" Dr. Featherstone asked wearily.

"The west, where the dominant element is fire. As we might expect, the land is excessively hot and dry, with a burning sun that never sets and casts a red hue on everything. Water is scarce and crops wither. This part of the kingdom is surrounded by a ring of steep impassable mountains and is called—appropriately enough—Blood Mountain. Those who have tried to cross the mountain range have fallen to their deaths or been killed by the savage giants who live there."

No one spoke for a moment. Beatrice was waiting for Dr. Featherstone to realize that it was laughable to think that Beatrice and her friends stood a chance against dragons, giants, werewolves, and sea monsters!

"So that's the order in which the regions must be entered," Dr. Featherstone murmured. "Winter Wood first. Then the south, then the east, then the west. And at that point, Beatrice and her party can enter Bromwich's castle?"

Dr. Meadowmouse nodded. "With the enchanted moat, a thirty-foot stone wall, and armed goblins—"

"Yes, Leopold," Dr. Featherstone said curtly. "We *understand* that each part of this will present challenges. But what is it they must do after they've made it past the barricades and obstacles?"

"They must find Bromwich's daughter. In the case of Winter Wood, that will be Rhona. They must find Rhona, and in her presence speak the words that will end the curse."

"What words?" Beatrice wanted to know.

"The words written here," Dr. Meadowmouse said. "They mustn't be spoken aloud until you are in the presence of Bromwich's daughter, and finally, with Bromwich himself. And only you may speak them, as the eldest female Bailiwick witch in this generation."

Dr. Featherstone was watching Beatrice closely.

"Suppose," Beatrice said slowly, "that we're able to get around the enchanted thorn hedge that surrounds Winter Wood. Somehow. And suppose we can avoid the fire-breathing dragon that guards Rhona. And suppose I can speak the words in her presence to break the spell. What happens then?"

"Let me see," Dr. Meadowmouse murmured, his eyes darting down the page. "Well, the snow and ice will melt, crops will grow, and evil will be banished. That means that Dally Rumpe will never be able to set foot on that land or cast any spells there again. Winter Wood will be forever free of him. *But,*" Dr. Meadowmouse added, "the other four regions will remain enchanted until each is entered and the counterspell repeated. Only after the spells on all five parts of Bailiwick have been broken will Bromwich be freed and the kingdom be whole again. And only then will Dally Rumpe lose all his powers and disappear forever."

"I see," Beatrice said. She looked at Teddy. "Do you still want to do this?"

Teddy hesitated for only an instant. Then she nodded yes decisively.

"Cyrus?"

He grinned and said, "Do you think I'd stay home and let you guys have all the fun?"

Beatrice caught Ollie's eye.

"If you go, I go," Ollie said.

Beatrice sighed. "Then let's plan to leave next Saturday."

Dr. Featherstone looked as though she had expected this all along. "Peregrine will escort you to the Witches' Sphere," she said. "Please show them the map, Peregrine."

The small witch reached inside his robes and pulled out a piece of parchment tied with black silk cord. He unrolled the map carefully and spread it out across Mr. Bailey's desk. Everyone closed in to peer at it.

"Here you can see the five parts of the kingdom," Dr. Featherstone said, "split apart as they are now. And there's Winter Wood."

To the west of Winter Wood, Beatrice noticed a crude drawing of a building with the words *Skull House* printed beneath it. "What is this?" she asked.

"Peregrine will take you there," Dr. Featherstone said, which didn't answer Beatrice's question at all.

"And before you go, you must read this book," Dr. Meadowmouse told her. "There's so much to do, you should understand it fully before you leave."

"There is a lot to do," Beatrice said. "How can we possibly accomplish it all in a week? That's all we have for Fall Break."

"What *is* this Fall Break you keep mentioning?" Dr. Featherstone asked impatiently. Without giving anyone time to answer, she said, "You'll do as much as you can do, one piece at a time. Bailiwick has been enchanted for two hundred years—the spells won't be broken overnight."

"And a week in mortal time is much longer in our sphere," Dr. Meadowmouse added kindly. "Time can be *streeeeeetched* as long as need be." And to demonstrate the point, he stretched his neck until his head was bumping against the ceiling like a helium-filled balloon.

Beatrice and her friends were taken aback by this display. Cyrus began to laugh.

"Behave yourself, Leopold," Dr. Featherstone said sternly, and muttered, "Show-off."

Dr. Meadowmouse came back to earth, looking delighted with himself.

Dr. Featherstone was studying Beatrice's worried face. "I know you have reservations, my dear, but you'll never learn what you can do until you try. And remember, it takes more than spells to create magic."

Mrs. Bailey squeezed Beatrice's arm. "Haven't I always told you that, sweetheart?"

Dr. Featherstone said, "And you were always right, Mrs. Bailey."

"What else does it take to create magic?" Beatrice asked.

"Courage, for one thing," Dr. Featherstone said.

"And caring," Dr. Meadowmouse added.

"And perseverance." This came from Peregrine, and they were all so surprised to hear him speak, they stared at him until he turned red and ducked his head.

"That's correct, Peregrine," Dr. Featherstone agreed. "No witch ever succeeded who gave up after the first try."

Peregrine looked up shyly, and the turned-down corners of his mouth turned up a little.

"Do you have any instructions for Beatrice before we go?" Dr. Featherstone asked him.

"I made a list," Peregrine said softly. He withdrew a wrinkled sheet of paper from a pocket in his robes and handed it to Beatrice.

Beatrice looked down at the paper. It read:

LIST

1. Pack only one bag that you would be able to carry on a long hike.
2. Bring a flashlight and extra batteries.
3. Wear comfortable clothes and shoes.
4. Bring a heavy jacket, gloves, and hat.

And at the bottom of the page, Peregrine had written:

Be ready to leave at 7:00 A.M. mortal time.
We have a long way to go.

It was nearly dawn when the last guests left the Bailey house. The party had been much more exciting than any of them had anticipated. Mr. and Mrs. Bailey went off to bed, yawning and wishing Beatrice a happy birthday, but Beatrice was too charged up to sleep. As was Teddy, who volunteered to stay and help her friend clean up.

Beatrice was stuffing wads of crepe paper into a trash bag when she said suddenly, "You're the one who's always wanted to be a Classical witch, not me. I thought I'd be a librarian. Or maybe a veterinarian."

"I don't begrudge you this opportunity, if that's what you're worried about," Teddy said. "And thanks to you, *I* get a second chance."

"You aren't scared?"

"Of course I am," Teddy said, sounding unreasonably cheerful.

Beatrice looked around at the dozens of half-filled glasses, the piles of paper plates and balled-up napkins, the chocolate cake ground into the rug, and frowned. Cleaning up would take them hours the regular way, and she was beginning to run out of steam. Beatrice started to chant:

> *Sweep and tidy,*
> *Mop and dust,*
> *Right this room*
> *Without a fuss.*

She had scarcely uttered the word *fuss*, when the trash bag lurched out of her hands and began to slide across the floor, banging into tables and sending figurines and glasses of witches' punch flying. At the same time, the broom was wrenched from Teddy's hands and began to swing at balloons and lampshades as if it were a baseball bat.

61

Beatrice grabbed the trash bag and struggled to hold onto it. Teddy went after the broom.

"Do you see why I'm worried?" Beatrice bellowed. "I can't even get a room-cleaning spell right!"

Teddy didn't have time to respond. She was vaulting over the back of the sofa in pursuit of the runaway broom.

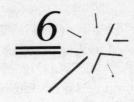

6

Under the Blackberry Bush

Beatrice had trouble concentrating that week. She went to her classes and tried to keep up with the assignments, but uppermost in her mind was the fact that she would soon be leaving for a place where dragons and giants walked the earth. Beatrice was so preoccupied, she barely noticed that Amanda Bugg and Jason Twitchel and their crowd were watching her more closely, gathering in the hall to whisper excitedly and then becoming tight-lipped and silent when she passed by.

After her last class on Wednesday, Beatrice was at her locker when she heard her name spoken above the babble of voices that filled the hall. She looked up and saw Olivia Klink and Shannon Doolittle standing nearby at Shannon's locker. They had their backs to Beatrice and apparently hadn't seen her.

"It was just on the Baileys' street," Olivia was saying in a loud voice. "Two feet of snow! I might have thought it was one of Amanda's tales, but my aunt saw it, too. She called my mom right away."

"I've always thought Beatrice Bailey was weird," Shannon said. "Remember in kindergarten when Mrs. Maudling asked us to name things you'd find in the kitchen?"

Olivia's laugh came out as a snort. "And Beatrice named a cauldron!"

Shannon started laughing, too. "And remember how Mrs. Maudling's face got pale and she started stuttering when she tried to explain to the rest of us what a cauldron was?"

"And in first grade—when we were jumping rope?" Olivia burst into a fit of giggles.

Shannon hooted. "Yeah—and Beatrice—"

"—came up with that bizarre rhyme—"

"And Julia Moody got so upset, she wet her pants!"

Olivia and Shannon doubled over, howling and holding their stomachs. They were creating such a scene, other students paused to stare and grin at them.

Beatrice had heard enough. Jaw clenched and lips pressed tightly together, she marched over to Shannon's locker.

Shannon saw her coming. She took one look at Beatrice's angry face, and her laughter died. The merriment and all color drained from her face. Gulping hard, Shannon jerked on Olivia's sleeve.

"What was that rhyme?" Olivia was wiping her eyes and leaning against the wall of lockers for support. "It was something about a witch." Olivia started giggling again. "A little bitty witch."

"Olivia," Shannon said sharply.

But before she could say anymore, Beatrice began to recite softly:

Little witch, little witch, fly around;
Elves and goblins live underground;
Ghosts and ghoulies shriek and groan,
Little witch, little witch, fly away home.

Olivia froze as she recognized the words from the rope-skipping rhyme. She turned around slowly when Beatrice finished, with the anxious look of someone who was trying to think fast.

"Oh—hi, Beatrice," Olivia said weakly. "I didn't see you there. Did you see her, Shannon?"

Shannon just stared nervously at Beatrice and didn't answer.

"I'm glad you remember all the fun times we had together," Beatrice said in a cold voice.

Olivia looked as though she intended to say something, but Beatrice turned away abruptly. She didn't want them to see the tears that had sprung unexpectedly to her eyes.

Beatrice was in her room memorizing counterspells from *The Bailiwick Family History* when her friends arrived. Ollie sat down on the floor beside Beatrice and started reading over her shoulder. Cyrus turned on the computer to play games. Teddy flopped down on Beatrice's bed and pulled a fashion magazine from her backpack. For the next five minutes, she wondered aloud about what clothes she should take to the Witches' Sphere.

"Good grief!" Cyrus said finally. "Who cares what you wear?"

"I don't want those Traditional witches thinking less of Reforms than they already do," Teddy said defensively. "We need to blend in."

"We *need* to make everything fit in one bag," Cyrus reminded her, "not a trunk."

Beatrice looked up from the lengthy spell she was trying to learn. "Will you two quit squabbling?" she demanded. "I'm having a breakdown over here."

"Sorry," Teddy murmured, and went back to looking at fall fashions in *Traditional Witch*.

It wasn't long before Beatrice slammed the book shut. "I'll never memorize all this in two days."

"You will," Teddy assured her. "By the way, did I tell you it's official? I can go."

Beatrice twisted around to stare at her. "Was there ever a doubt?"

Teddy grinned. "Not really. I just had to wear my pop down. He was a little concerned, but he knew he'd never hear the end of it if he didn't let me go."

"My folks said okay after my mom talked to Beatrice's mother for an hour," Cyrus said. "She felt better when she found out we'd have adult supervision."

"You mean Peregrine?" Ollie laughed.

"We'll probably be taking care of *him*," Beatrice predicted, "not the other way around."

"He may not be the *best* witch adviser there ever was," Cyrus agreed cheerfully, "but he had to have *something* going for him to be selected, didn't he?"

"I just had a terrible thought." Beatrice frowned. "What if *we're* Peregrine's test?"

Teddy started to laugh, then broke off abruptly. "You know, Beatrice, you might have something there."

"What about you, Ollie?" Beatrice asked. "Any problems with your folks?"

"Are you joking? My father said I was to go and make a fine showing of myself or he'd never be able to hold his head up at the club again." Ollie's smile was strained. "He plays golf with these guys whose children are brilliant witches."

"But I bet none of them has ever fought dragons and werewolves," Beatrice said, smiling.

"They've been so deprived," Ollie said drily.

Beatrice went over to her closet and pulled out a large backpack. "I guess I'd better think about packing."

"All you need is a toothbrush and a change of underwear," Cyrus said.

"A change?" Teddy wrinkled up her nose. "Remind me to steer clear of you after the first day."

Beatrice dug around in a dresser drawer until she found a flashlight and a small compass. "Ollie, why don't you read the part about Winter Wood aloud?" she suggested.

Ollie had just started to read when he was interrupted by a clank and a clatter.

"Oh, no," Beatrice said.

Ollie looked up. "What's wrong?"

"I dropped my compass. I think it went into this heat vent on the floor."

Teddy leaned off the bed and peered through the grate. "Yep, I see it. How do you take off this cover?"

"I don't know." Beatrice got down on her hands and knees and tried to remove the grate. "It's stuck. And my hand won't fit through the openings."

"That's okay," Cyrus said. "I'll get it."

He walked over to the vent and started to mumble:

> By the mysteries, one and all,
> Make me shrink from tall to small.
> Cut me down to inches three,
> As my will, so mote it be.

Instantly, Cyrus began to shrink smaller and smaller, until he was only three inches tall.

Teddy shook her head. "I never get used to seeing him do that."

Cyrus sat down on the grate and lowered himself slowly through one of the openings.

"Be careful," Beatrice called after him.

There was a dull thud when Cyrus landed on the narrow ledge where the compass rested.

"This is heavier than it looks," came Cyrus's tiny voice. With a grunt, he lifted the compass over his head.

Beatrice grabbed it. "Thanks, Cyrus. Can you get out?"

"Sure."

Cyrus took hold of the grate and hoisted himself up through the vent. Once out, he began to chant:

> By the mysteries, one and all,
> Make me grow from small to tall.

Let me from this spell be free,
As my will, so mote it be.

And he was suddenly his normal size again.

"Sorry to put you to so much trouble," Beatrice said.

"Keeps me in shape," Cyrus said cheerfully. "Magically speaking, that is. What a shame if I forgot the only spell I know how to cast, right?"

Beatrice stuffed a nightgown into her backpack. "So everybody's sure about this?" she asked. "It's not too late to back out."

Teddy had moved to Beatrice's dressing table and was looking through a box of costume jewelry. "I'm absolutely sure," she said, pulling on a bangle bracelet and holding out her hand to admire it.

"Me, too," Cyrus said. "I need some excitement in my life."

"I've read about dark magic and evil spells," Ollie said thoughtfully, "but seeing it firsthand should add a new dimension."

"A new dimension," Beatrice muttered, and crammed some socks into her bag.

At seven o'clock on Saturday morning, Peregrine showed up in the front hall. He didn't ring the bell, and no one saw a ball of light. He was suddenly just there.

Mr. Bailey was carrying Beatrice's backpack down the stairs, and Mrs. Bailey was handing out lunches to Beatrice, Cyrus, and Ollie. Teddy hadn't arrived yet.

"Here, Peregrine, one for you, too," Mrs. Bailey said.

The witch adviser took the brown bag, and Beatrice thought she saw him well up. "Thank you very much," he mumbled, and sniffed.

Mrs. Bailey's eyes fell on Beatrice's backpack. "Did you remember gloves and a hat?" She tried to sound casual, but didn't succeed. After all, Beatrice was her only child, and she wasn't heading off to Girl Scout camp.

"I did, Mom," Beatrice said, then added, "Don't worry, okay?"

"Of *course* I'll worry!"

They gathered up their bags and moved out to the porch. The sun was just beginning to come up over the trees, and the air was still frosty.

Beatrice looked at her watch. "Seven ten. I wonder where Teddy is."

"There," Cyrus said, pointing to the street.

They all looked. Teddy was wearing long black robes and dragging an overstuffed wheeled suitcase down the street behind her.

Cyrus hooted. "I *knew* it! Didn't I say she'd bring everything she owns?"

"And look at the getup she's wearing," Ollie said. "Will she be able to hike in that?"

"In a word, *no*," Beatrice said.

Teddy was entering the front yard, but the suitcase wouldn't roll across the grass. She pulled and tugged, then looked helplessly at the watchers on the porch.

Mr. Bailey went to assist her.

"Have you got a pair of jeans in that thing?" Beatrice shouted. "Well, get them and come inside with me."

A few minutes later, an annoyed Teddy came out of the house wearing jeans and carrying one of Beatrice's old backpacks over her shoulder. "You're so mean to make me leave everything," she grumbled to her friend.

"You couldn't possibly walk with that suitcase."

"*Walk!*" Teddy said in dismay. "But we're witches! On a Noble Quest. I thought we'd *fly* or something."

"You didn't read my list," Peregrine said, looking as though his feelings were hurt.

"I did," Teddy said hastily. "I must have—overlooked that part." She kicked at the porch railing and scowled. "Anyhow, I'm ready. With nothing decent to wear, and looking like a *mortal*! Let's get this show on the road."

Mr. Bailey hugged Beatrice. "Your mother and I will be proud of you whether you break the spell or not," he said gruffly. "Be careful, and don't take any unnecessary chances."

"I won't," Beatrice promised.

"And be home by Halloween," Mrs. Bailey said. "We've never been apart on Halloween."

Then everyone was hugging and kissing and saying good-bye. Mr. and Mrs. Bailey stood on the front steps, watching and waving, as Peregrine led Beatrice and her friends around the side of the house and into the backyard.

Beatrice reached into the pocket of her bag and brought out an area map. She ran to catch up with Peregrine, who was walking fast and looking straight ahead.

"Where is Bailiwick, anyway?" she asked him. "If we're walking, it must be nearby."

"Relatively."

"But *where*? I pored over this map for hours, and I couldn't find it."

"You won't find Bailiwick on a mortal's map," Peregrine said, glancing shyly at her. "It's in the Witches' Sphere."

They were passing the pumpkin patch. Sunlight was already melting frost from the pumpkins and bathing them in a fiery glow. A small brown hare peeked out from the tangle of vines to watch them go by.

When they came to the back of the lot, where ferns and blackberry bushes grew wild, Peregrine stopped. He reached out and parted the thorny branches of one of the bushes. Beneath it was the opening to a tunnel.

"I didn't know this was here!" Beatrice exclaimed.

"That's not surprising," Peregrine said. "They're always changing the ramps to the Witches' Sphere. Under Construction signs everywhere you look these days. Very confusing."

Just then, Beatrice noticed Cayenne heading for the tunnel entrance.

"Oh, no, you don't." Beatrice bent down and grabbed the cat. "You can't go, Cay. It's too dangerous."

Peregrine was watching her out of the corner of his eye. "You're a witch," he said.

"Uh—yes."

"And this cat, I presume, is your familiar?"

"I suppose so." Beatrice was wondering where this was leading.

"A witch's familiar normally accompanies its witch on quests and adventures. That's the *point* of a familiar," Peregrine added, staring hard at his feet while his ears turned pink. "To be of assistance to its witch. Your cat is just trying to do its job."

Cayenne had been gazing steadily at Beatrice. Now Cayenne spoke with a soft but emphatic, "Meooow."

"Well," Beatrice said, "I didn't know. I'm new at this. Okay, you can come," she said to Cayenne, "but don't wander off where I can't see you."

The cat jumped down, and Beatrice turned to thank Peregrine for educating her. But the witch adviser wasn't there.

Then Beatrice saw one of his skinny feet—just before it disappeared into the tunnel under the blackberry bush.

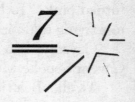

The Witches' Sphere

"*T*urn on your flashlights," Peregrine said.

Four lights came on, then a fifth. Peregrine was wearing a hard hat with a bright light attached. Beatrice thought he looked like some strange kind of miner.

At first, they had to crawl on their hands and knees, which was hard to do with flashlights and backpacks. Then the burrow began to expand, until they could finally stand up straight and walk. It was a narrow passage cut through rock and clay and smelled of damp earth. Even with their lights shining, the tunnel was dark and shadowy. And it curved often, making it impossible to see more than a few yards ahead.

Beatrice didn't notice anyone else, so she thought they must be alone in the tunnel. But then she began to hear noises nearby: pebbles bouncing against stone, as if someone had kicked them loose; a gentle rustling that suggested movement—whether human or not she couldn't tell; and finally, whispering. Yes—it was definitely the sound of voices, but they were so soft, she couldn't make out what was being said.

Beatrice quickened her pace until she was just behind Peregrine. "Someone else is here," she said softly.

"Of course," Peregrine said. "This *is* a public highway."

Perhaps her eyes were beginning to adjust to the dim light. Or maybe the other travelers on the underground road had grown accustomed to Beatrice and her companions, and were more willing to show themselves. In any case, Beatrice began to see them. Little people no larger than grasshoppers walked along the sides of the tunnel. They wore peaked hats and tiny stockings that wouldn't stay up on their broomstraw legs and puddled around their ankles. There were some with wings who darted within inches of Beatrice's face and then flew away down the passage.

"What are they?" Beatrice whispered to Peregrine.

"Why, they're fairies." He was so surprised by the question that he forgot to duck his head and looked her straight in the face. "Don't you have fairies in your garden at home?"

"Not that I've seen," Beatrice replied.

Suddenly she noticed Cayenne lurking behind a rock, apparently ready to pounce on some unsuspecting fairies who had stopped to rest. Beatrice picked up the cat and, to Cayenne's chagrin, placed her in a large pocket in the backpack.

"I knew bringing you was a bad idea," Beatrice muttered. She zipped the pocket shut so that only Cayenne's head was visible.

They had been walking a long time, and were beginning to grow tired, when Peregrine pointed out a doorway carved into the rock. "We should stop at this rest area," he said. "There won't be another one for miles."

They followed him through the opening and found themselves in a large cave that was illuminated by dozens of burning torches.

"Rest rooms that way," Peregrine said, indicating a passageway. Then he pointed to the rear of the cave, where water trickled down jagged rocks into a clear pool. Bushes and vines covered with berries grew nearby. "Refreshments there," he said.

An old man in dark green robes was sitting at the edge of the pool catching water in his cupped hands. He drank noisily. Then he noticed them staring and grinned. "Help yourselves," he said. "There's plenty for everyone."

"Look at the raspberries," Cyrus said. "And blackberries and blueberries."

"And strawberries, too," Teddy said.

"All ripe at the same time?" Ollie asked.

"Why not?" the old man countered.

Beatrice started to ask him how that was possible, and how berries could grow underground at all without sunlight—but the old man had vanished.

"Was he a witch?" Beatrice asked Peregrine.

"He was," Peregrine said, apparently still mystified because she couldn't identify magic-folk any better than she could. "And so are they," he added, as two middle-aged women entered the cave, deep in conversation and not paying any attention to Beatrice and the others.

"And they're wearing *robes* and *witches' hats*," Teddy said in consternation.

They ate the lunches Mrs. Bailey had prepared, and stuffed themselves with berries—which they all agreed were better than any they had ever tasted in the mortal world. Beatrice allowed Cayenne to stretch her legs and fed the cat bits of tuna from her own sandwich.

When they returned to the tunnel, it was teeming with witches and fairies, which Beatrice was now able to recognize. A while later, they came to a sign that read: *The Borderlands—Next 5 Exits*. Peregrine turned off at Exit 2.

The ramp was narrow and littered with loose pebbles. They had to take care not to scrape their elbows on the stone sides or lose their footing. Then the passageway began to slant upward, becoming very steep and difficult to climb.

"How much farther?" Teddy asked, panting.

"We're nearly there," Peregrine said. "See the light up ahead?"

They moved doggedly toward the point of light. Finally, breathless and weary, they stumbled into the outside world. Dazed by the brilliance, and too tired to take another step, they fell to the ground.

When her eyes had become accustomed to the sunlight, Beatrice blew her bangs aside and looked around. Green fields stretched as far as she could see, dipping into valleys, then rising into gentle hills. A packed-earth road, just wide enough for three to walk abreast, wound around the hills and into the valleys. Shade trees grew alongside the road and primroses formed untidy hedges.

It's beautiful and peaceful here, Beatrice thought, *but nothing out of the ordinary.* She assumed they must still be in the mortal world, but then she noticed the light—a quivering yellow radiance that seemed to turn everything it touched to gold. And there was the music the wind made blowing through the tall grass; it might have been a flute playing, the melody as sweet and tender as a lullaby. Green fields and golden light. Flute music. Goose bumps popped up on Beatrice's arms. She shivered, even though the sun was warm. This place—it was almost like her dream. But not quite. The grass wasn't as brilliantly green, and the light wasn't as intense. But there were too many similarities for this to be a coincidence. Beatrice's heart began to thump, then pound, as she realized that they must be near the magical place she had seen in her dreams.

"You're in The Borderlands," Peregrine told them. "Between the mortal world and the Witches' Sphere. Come on," he said. "We've rested long enough."

They followed Peregrine down the road and met other witches in brightly colored robes and hats. Some were walking, but most whizzed past on brooms, and one was riding sidesaddle on a white horse. Fairies flew by, and a few wingless ones rode on the backs of butterflies.

After a while, Peregrine said, "We're coming to the border crossing."

Just ahead, a gray stone wall rose twenty feet into the air. There was an opening for the road to run through, with a wooden gate topped by strands of barbed wire. Standing in front of the gate were two of the ugliest creatures Beatrice had ever seen.

"I *know* you won't have observed any of *these* in your

backyard," Peregrine said under his breath. "They're troll guards."

The trolls were horrible. Beatrice peered at them from behind Peregrine as he walked stalwartly toward the gate. They were at least eight feet tall, and as big around as four normal people. Wearing filthy rags, with gray caps pulled down over their greasy hair, the trolls had squinty suspicious eyes and mean-looking mouths. And they were near enough now for Beatrice to notice that they had a *very* bad odor.

"Follow me and don't say anything," Peregrine said softly.

He walked up to one of the guards. Beatrice and her friends stayed close behind.

Peregrine retrieved a piece of paper from inside his robes and handed it to the troll. "Here's my pass," he said.

As scared as she was, Beatrice still noticed that her witch adviser didn't appear timid at all. He spoke with authority. Even so, the troll glowered at him before looking down at the paper.

"As you can see, it's signed by the director of the Witches' Institute," Peregrine said. "I have permission to cross into the Witches' Sphere with four witches and a familiar." Peregrine turned Beatrice around and pointed to Cayenne, who took one look at the troll and slid down as far as she could into her pocket. Peregrine turned Beatrice forward again.

The troll squinted unpleasantly at Beatrice and her friends. The second troll lumbered over and did the same. Then he leaned down into Beatrice's face and leered at her. He was drooling, and his breath was atrocious.

"We don't have all day," Peregrine snapped. "I wouldn't want to have to report you for inefficiency. Open the gate, please."

The trolls growled and muttered and glared at Peregrine, but they moved heavily toward the gate and pulled it open. Still grumbling, they waved the group through.

Beatrice and her companions walked quickly and silently down the road until the border guards were out of sight. That's when Peregrine began to tremble. His hands and his arms and his legs—and even his skinny feet—started to quiver. Beatrice realized suddenly that he was about to collapse and reached out to catch him.

"So embarrassing," he mumbled. "Trolls always effect me this way. So sorry," he said, glancing at Beatrice, then looking at the ground. "Didn't mean to fall apart like this."

"You were wonderful," Beatrice assured him, trying to hold him up as he twitched and shivered.

Cyrus and Ollie came to help Beatrice support the witch adviser.

"You were so brave," Teddy said.

Ollie and Cyrus agreed that he was nothing short of heroic.

The reassurance must have worked because the trembling and twitching lessened, and finally Peregrine was able to stand on his own. "Thank you, thank you," he said, waving his hand like a fan in front of his damp, flushed face. "So kind of you to say."

They made him sit down and collect himself. After a short rest, he stood up, once more steady on his feet, and said, "It's not much farther. We want to get there before dark."

"Absolutely," Beatrice said. She had no idea where they were going, but she didn't intend to sleep out on the road with those border guards roaming around.

"Welcome to the Witches' Sphere," Peregrine said, and for the first time since they had met him, he smiled. It was just a sliver of a smile, and a little crooked, but it warmed Beatrice all the way to her toes. She realized that she was growing fond of her witch adviser.

The countryside was wild and scary on this side of the wall. The roadsides were heavily wooded, with dark trees looming over them and shutting out the light. The ground was covered with a dense growth of tangled vines and prickly bushes. Beyond the woods, jagged mountain peaks were silhouetted against black storm clouds.

"This part of the Witches' Sphere is called The Barrens," Peregrine said. "I suppose you can see why."

Teddy was looking around at the dark forest with anxious eyes. "Then it isn't all like this?"

"Goodness, no," Peregrine said. "Some areas have even been overdeveloped. We have cities as modern as those in the mortal world, with malls and pollution and everything."

Teddy perked up. "Are we going to a place with a mall?"

"Well, no," Peregrine said. Then he added, "Most Traditional witches prefer the clean air and privacy of The Barrens."

As the road wound deeper into the forest, Beatrice began to feel as if they were being watched. Several times, she thought she saw eyes glowing among the trees. But when she looked more closely, the eyes disappeared.

The trees began to thin out. Peregrine finally led them from the forest, and they came to stand at the edge of a cliff. Brown fields spread out for miles at their feet. The road slithered down the side of the embankment, then meandered across the fields toward the mountains. The landscape was bleak, Beatrice reflected, and apparently uninhabited.

Then she saw the house.

Still some distance away, it was built of gray stone, with arched windows and balconies and a circular tower at each of its four corners. The house wasn't exactly a castle, but it was close enough for Beatrice.

"That stone house down the road is our destination," Peregrine told them.

Beatrice was thrilled. She couldn't wait to see inside an almost castle.

"It's called Skull House," Peregrine said.

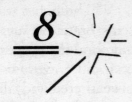

Skull House

Beatrice had wondered what Skull House was since she noticed it on the Bailiwick map the night of her birthday party. Now she was about to find out.

As they walked down the road toward the house, Beatrice could see that it was quite large. The main structure was three stories high, and each tower had an additional floor that rose above the rest of the house. The sign out front read: *Skull House Bed & Breakfast.*

"Bed & Breakfast?" Cyrus asked in surprise.

"Witches need to get away like everyone else," Peregrine pointed out.

He turned off the road and started down a flagstone walk that led to the house. The others followed. Now they could read the small print at the bottom of the sign: *The Weary Witch-Traveler's Home Away from Home.*

Certainly, this was no ordinary house. For one thing, the front door was set into a boulder. It seemed that the rest of the structure had been built around this enormous gray stone, which was shaped exactly like a skull. Beatrice hoped this accounted for the B&B's unusual name.

The house was surrounded by bare trees, their drooping branches suggesting a circle of melancholy guardians around the property. Adding to the sense of desolation was an old graveyard in a nearby field. The headstones were weathered and tilted at odd angles.

"That's the Bone Yard," Peregrine said.

Just then a whitish transparent shape floated out from behind a headstone. Beatrice had never seen a ghost, but she knew this had to be one. There were its arms and legs and head, and two black holes where eyes should have been. The ghost glided across the tops of the gravestones and then stopped. It seemed to be staring straight at Beatrice and her companions. The next thing they knew, the apparition was zooming through the air toward them. It came closer and closer, aimed for Teddy's face, and then—just before it reached her—the phantom veered sharply to the left and sped away.

Teddy screamed. Then she took a quick breath and giggled nervously. "I thought—I thought it was going to fly right through me," she gasped.

"Ghosts can be full of high spirits," Peregrine said, and the corners of his mouth turned up. "High *spirits*—heh-heh."

Teddy wasn't amused. She frowned at him.

Peregrine's mouth drooped again and he lowered his eyes. "Anyway," he said timidly, "the ghosts provide a lot of entertainment for the B&B guests."

"Do they always just *pop up* that way?" Cyrus asked.

"There's no need to be frightened," Peregrine said. "The *ghosts* won't hurt you."

"But something else might?" Ollie prodded.

Peregrine considered the question seriously. "There's a lot of good magic in and around Skull House," he said finally. "You *should* be protected from dark magic."

He means Dally Rumpe, Beatrice thought.

Peregrine confirmed this by adding, "But you need to stay alert. Don't think for a minute that the evil sorcerer isn't watching you. He might be close by even now, observing your every move. Be assured that he knows why you're here," Peregrine warned, "and will do whatever he can to stop you."

They had arrived at the dark red door embedded in the skull stone.

"Well, here you are," Peregrine said. "I'll come to escort you back to the mortal world after you've finished what you've come to do."

"*What!*" Beatrice couldn't believe she had heard correctly. "Surely you don't think you're leaving us here alone."

"You're her witch adviser," Ollie said. "Aren't you supposed to help her?"

"I've got tons of work back at the office," Peregrine said. "You aren't my only advisee, you know," he informed Beatrice. "Besides, this is *your* test. If I did all the work, it would be my test."

"And isn't it?" Teddy muttered.

"But we don't even know what to do first," Beatrice said. "How do we get started?"

"Oh, you'll be receiving instructions from the Witches' Executive Committee," Peregrine said hastily. "Did you think we'd expect you to take off on your own?"

"It sounded that way," Cyrus said.

"Oh, my, no," Peregrine responded, looking distressed. "Just wait for the instructions. They'll be coming via registered mail, and I'm sure you'll find them helpful. You mustn't do anything until they arrive."

"Don't worry," Beatrice said. She was feeling cranky.

"How long before the instructions arrive?" Ollie asked.

"A day," Peregrine said vaguely, "or two. Anyway, if you run into trouble, I can be here in a flash. Just tell the owner of the B&B that you need to send quick-mail to the Institute."

"How do we send—" Beatrice started.

But Peregrine had already opened the door for them. "Well, good-bye then," he said, and ducked his head. "Good luck to you all." And then he was gone. Vanished. Just like that.

The door opened wide with a groan. A very small man wearing a blue coat with tails, a yellow-checked vest, and a purple hat with a floppy brim glared up at them.

"Welcome to Skull House B&B," the man said grudgingly, scowling even more as he looked them up and down. "I'm Gus, official greeter and elf at your service."

So this was an elf. Beatrice made a mental note.

"Well, don't just stand there," Gus grumbled. "Come in if you're coming."

They entered a huge room with a gray stone floor and walls. To their right was a curving staircase that rose to a second-floor balcony. Facing the staircase was a long counter with rows of mail cubbies behind it. Chairs with dusty cushions and high carved backs, reminiscent of the Spanish Inquisition, were arranged in conversation areas.

"Leave your bags here," Gus ordered.

The elf jerked a bellpull on the wall. The tolling of a giant bell echoed through the room, startling Beatrice and her friends. They all jumped, and Beatrice fell back against a stone statue. When she looked up, she did a double take. It was a seven-foot sculpture of a gargoyle, with long fangs and beady eyes.

Gus was watching her.

"Nice," Beatrice said, patting the gargoyle's skinny arm.

She moved closer to her friends. They all looked anxiously around the lobby. Pentagrams were carved above the windows. Paintings of women and men in witches' robes lined the walls. Flickering candles from an enormous chandelier spilled light across the worn Oriental rugs, but the corners of the room remained hidden in shadow.

Beatrice noticed a cat with long golden fur lying on the front desk. The cat stood and stretched. It walked the length of the counter and rubbed its head against Beatrice's arm in a friendly way, then nudged an open guest book toward her.

"I guess he's telling us to sign it," Beatrice said.

Cayenne was crying and kicking to be freed. Beatrice lowered her backpack to the floor and unzipped her cat's traveling pocket. Cayenne stared up at the gold cat for a moment, then leaped onto the desk. The felines touched noses and sniffed.

Beatrice picked up a silver and ebony pen from the desk. The gold cat pushed a silver inkwell toward her. Beatrice dipped the pen into the ink and started to sign her name. But she had only written the B when the pen flew out of her hand and began to write on its own. Unnerved, Beatrice looked at the book and saw the name *Beatrice Bailiwick* written at the top of the page. It looked like her own handwriting.

Beatrice was astonished. She passed the pen to Teddy. "Try this," she said. "Once you write the first letter, it takes over and does the rest."

Teddy wrote a *T* and paused. Nothing happened. She wrote an *e*, then a *d*, then another *d*.

"The pen isn't magic for me," Teddy said, sounding very disappointed, and wrote her name with a sigh.

Ollie and Cyrus tried it, too, but the pen didn't finish their names, either.

"Well, it *is* your test," Ollie said to Beatrice.

Suddenly, a door at the back of the room opened and a gust of wind swept through, followed by a woman in long dark red robes. She was at least six feet tall, with broad shoulders and a strong ruddy face. Her brown hair was streaked with gray and fastened in a haphazard knot on top of her head.

The woman started toward them. She had a regal bearing, and her robes flowed beautifully as she walked. Then Beatrice looked down and saw that the woman was wearing a pair of dingy tennis shoes with holes in the toes.

The woman stopped in front of Beatrice and smiled warmly. "Has Wooly Mittens welcomed you?" she asked, glancing at the gold cat. "He manages the B&B. If you need anything during your stay, please don't hesitate to tell him. I'm the owner of Skull House. Genevieve Snapps. Neva."

"How do you do, Ms. Snapps?" Beatrice extended her hand.

The woman glanced at Beatrice's outstretched hand and frowned as though Beatrice had done something slightly vulgar. "Please," she said, "call me Neva, plain and simple."

"Neva Plain and Simple," Cyrus said, grinning. "What an unusual name."

Neva peered at Cyrus and frowned again. Then she said, "Gus, please take our guests to their rooms."

She looked around, but there was no Gus.

A female elf came through the door in the back wall. She looked very much like Gus, except that her blond hair was long and plaited into two braids, and she was wearing a blue dress with a red jacket. She was also smiling cheerfully.

"Birdella, where is Gus?" Neva asked.

"I'll find him, ma'am," the elf replied. "But shall I show the guests to their rooms first?"

"Please do," Neva said, looking annoyed. "And when you find Gus, tell him to take their bags upstairs."

Birdella had started for the stairs when a bloodcurdling scream sounded from somewhere above them.

Neva's face turned red and she bellowed, "*Stop that*, you scummy, scabby, despicable, little wretch!" She muttered under her breath, "I'll kill him. Well—I *would* kill him, if he weren't already dead."

Then Neva lifted her robes and bounded up the stairs with a murderous look in her eyes.

Beatrice and her friends stared after the woman and didn't move.

"That's Odd," Birdella said.

"It sure is," Beatrice agreed. "Everything about this place is odd."

"No," Birdella said quickly. "I mean, that screaming is coming from Odd Begley. He's a ghost."

Cyrus looked interested. "And he haunts Skull House?"

"He does," Birdella said. "Since last Tuesday. But it's not working out."

When Neva came back, she was puffing and panting. The knot of hair on top of her head was further askew and she had a dust bunny hanging from her right earlobe. She was talking to herself, and appeared very agitated, as she stomped down the stairs.

"I never should have taken him," Neva was saying. "All that screaming makes the guests nervous."

"You mean, you *agreed* to let him haunt your house?" Beatrice asked.

"Well, yes," Neva said. "He was haunting NBA Headquarters, and driving them crazy. I said I'd help out."

"He was haunting the National Basketball Association?" Ollie asked.

"*No!* The Nonsectarian Bewitchment Association." Neva looked suspiciously at Ollie. "Don't you belong? Anyway, with Odd moaning and screeching all the time, NBA members couldn't concentrate on their spells. He *had* to leave."

"Of course," Ollie said.

Beatrice just shook her head, thinking, *And Amanda Bugg thought my house was strange.*

9

Fair Warning!

"Come on then," Birdella said, smiling at Beatrice and her friends. "I'll take you to your rooms."

Beatrice started across the lobby, then stopped. There was activity under the stairs. Way back in the dark recesses something was thumping around. Then Beatrice saw a pair of eyes gleaming in the darkness.

Cayenne had leaped down from the desk to follow Beatrice. The cat stared for a moment into the gloom beneath the stairs, then she hissed.

"Oh, you've discovered Tom, have you?" Neva said.

"Who's Tom?" Beatrice asked. "Another ghost?"

"Actually, yes," Neva said.

"And he haunts Skull House?"

"Actually, no. Trembling Tom is his full name," Neva said. "He's too much of a scaredy cat to haunt anything."

Beatrice looked closer at the two glowing eyes. She could just make out the wispy outline of a small animal. A rounded head, two pointed ears—"Is Trembling Tom *literally* a cat?" Beatrice asked.

"Isn't that what I just said?" Neva asked impatiently. "At least, he's the ghost of a cat. Wooly Mittens brought him home weeks ago, but he's too timid to let himself be seen."

Birdella led them up the wide curving stairs, down a hallway, and up another staircase. This one was narrow and creaky and swayed as though it might not hold up under their weight. They walked the length of another hall, and then up another narrow flight of stairs.

"Wooly Mittens thought you'd like tower rooms," Birdella said, taking them down another corridor. "More atmospheric, you know."

They came to a massive oak door.

"Here you are, ladies. Your room is in the East Tower," Birdella said. "The gentlemen will be around the corner in the West Tower."

Birdella opened the door, and Cayenne ran into the room.

"There's a bath next door," Birdella said. "You'll find plenty of towels. Dinner's at seven in the dining room off the lobby."

"I didn't know B&Bs served dinner," Teddy said.

Birdella looked at Teddy as if she were simpleminded. "And just where else would a witch have dinner around here?" Birdella asked. "The closest diner's halfway across the sphere."

Just then Gus arrived dragging the girls' bags behind him. He was out of breath and looking crabbier than ever. "An elevator," he grumbled. "Would that be too much to ask?"

"Thank you, Gus," Teddy said.

Beatrice dug into the pocket of her jeans and brought

out two crumpled bills, which she handed to the elf. He scowled and slapped the money back into Beatrice's hand.

"Mortal tender! What good is *that* going to do me?" Gus demanded, and stomped out the door.

Birdella looked embarrassed. "I suppose it *is* a long way to carry bags," she said. Then, all brisk efficiency again, she added, "I'll show you gentlemen to your rooms now."

Beatrice and Teddy followed Cayenne into a large round room. They stared in amazement at two gigantic beds that had been intricately carved to look like magical creatures. One was a dragon, the other a lion-headed griffin.

Beatrice walked over to the dragon bed. Its head and its clawed front feet formed the headboard. The footboard was composed of the dragon's back feet and long curving tail. The creature seemed to be lying on its back holding a feather mattress to its belly.

"Incredible," Beatrice said. "Can I have the dragon?"

The boys stopped by to get Beatrice and Teddy for dinner. Cyrus walked in, saw the beds, and grinned. "We wondered if you had them, too. Aren't they wild?"

"I'll be sleeping on some sort of sea monster," Ollie said. "And Cyrus's bed looks remarkably like our friendly border guards."

Suddenly the giant bell tolled, causing Beatrice and her friends to clamp their hands over their ears. Even so, their heads were still ringing when they finally made their way down three hallways and as many staircases to the lobby.

A sign printed with the words *Dining Room* pointed to the door in the back wall. As they headed toward the door,

Beatrice was certain that they were being watched. Just as she reached the door, she spun around—and caught a blur as something sprinted under the stairs.

"Tom?" Beatrice called softly, but there was no response.

Birdella met them as they entered the dining room. "This way," she said, and led them to a corner table. "You can see everything from here," she said eagerly. "You know, soak up local color, it being your first time in the sphere and all."

"How did you know this is our first trip to the Witches' Sphere?" Ollie asked.

Birdella looked surprised by the question. "There aren't many secrets at Skull House," she said.

There were five chairs at the table. Cayenne jumped into one of them without hesitation.

Beatrice looked from Cayenne to Birdella. "Is that all right?" she asked.

"And why wouldn't it be?" Birdella replied. "She's a cat, after all."

Wooly Mittens was wandering among the tables, looking up as if to see that everyone's needs were being met. An attractive young woman with short dark hair was taking the order of a distinguished-looking man in gray robes. The man had removed his hat and placed it on the chair beside him. His silver hair gleamed in the candlelight. Beatrice noticed the hat at once because there were gold stars and crescent moons scattered across the gray silk background.

"That's Most Worthy Piddle," Birdella said, following Beatrice's gaze. There was a note of pride in her voice.

"Who's Most Worthy—whatever you said?" Beatrice asked.

Birdella stared at her. "Are you serious? You really don't *know*? Why he's just one of the most celebrated witches there is," she said, growing agitated. "A great scholar. He's done important research and lectures at Witch U. He's a world-renowned witch tutor."

"Oh."

"A *great* witch," Birdella said again, still looking distressed when she left.

Cyrus grinned. "Make a note," he said to Beatrice. "Elves are sensitive about their heros."

"So I see."

The pretty waitress came over to their table. "Good evening," she said, smiling. "I'm Amarantha, and I'll be your server."

She handed them menus that had been hand printed on old parchment, and chanted pleasantly:

> *Heat of flame, glow of fire,*
> *To light this candle is my desire.*

A flame appeared on the candle in the center of their table.

"Take your time deciding," Amarantha said. "I highly recommend the house specialty—fennel salad with serpent's-tooth dressing."

She left and went to a table where a pale young woman in sensible navy robes seemed to be falling asleep over her soup bowl.

"Will you look at this menu," Teddy whispered. "It's unbelievable."

"No burgers," Cyrus said mournfully. "No pizza."

Ollie grinned. "Must you be so mortal, Cyrus? Live dangerously! Try the bat-claw soup or the sweet rice with mouse whiskers."

"Not on your life," Cyrus growled.

"I just thought of something," Beatrice said. "How are we going to pay for this? If Gus's reaction is any indication, they don't seem to appreciate mortal money here."

"No problem," Ollie said. "Look at your menus."

When the other three complied, they saw that spidery writing had suddenly appeared below the list of desserts.

"*Meals, lodging, and entertainment,*" Beatrice read, "*are free to everyone in the Bailiwick party. Bon appétit!*"

"All right!" Cyrus exclaimed. Then he looked crestfallen. "I can have anything I want—but I don't want anything on this menu. What kind of deal is that?"

He was eventually persuaded to try a green herb omelette and lemon-balm cheesecake. The others were more adventurous. They ordered everything from dragon's-breath soup to roasted lizard's tongue.

Beatrice had been filling a bowl with tasty morsels from her own plate for Cayenne when Amarantha appeared with a plate for the cat. "Salmon cooked with rosemary," she said. "Compliments of Wooly Mittens."

Cayenne began to nibble delicately at the salmon and purr. Soon the cat's body started to vibrate and she forgot everything she had ever known about dainty table manners.

Beatrice laughed. "Please thank Wooly Mittens for Cayenne," she told Amarantha.

While sipping their after-dinner witches' brew, they had a chance to look around at their fellow diners. At a table nearby were a nice-looking young man and woman, the only ones there besides Beatrice's group who weren't attired in witches' robes. The couple wore walking shorts and thick-soled lace-up boots. It looked as though they intended to do some serious hiking.

Then Beatrice noticed a donkey standing at one of the tables—and did a double take. No, her eyes hadn't deceived her. It was a large dark brown donkey chowing down on a platter heaped with sage oatcakes.

"That's Crispin," Amarantha said, "one of Neva's strays. Isn't he adorable?"

"So Neva takes in stray animals," Teddy said.

"Oh, Crispin isn't an animal," Amarantha replied. "He's a witch, but he's been enchanted. Neva says it was a former girlfriend in a fit of jealousy. Poor Crispin's stuck with being a donkey until the spell expires in another fifty or sixty years. Actually," Amarantha added thoughtfully, "he doesn't seem to mind as long as his meals are served on time."

After everyone had finished eating, Neva swept dramatically into the dining room. She had changed into black silk robes for evening. "There's a party outside," she said. "With entertainment and more witches' brew. Amarantha will show you the way."

"We should probably go to bed early," Ollie said. "We'll need to be rested in case our instructions from the Witches' Executive Committee come in the morning."

"But we can't miss our first party in the Witches' Sphere," Teddy protested.

Beatrice agreed. "We could stay a little while and still get a good night's sleep."

They followed Amarantha down a hallway lined with portraits of more witches and out the back door into the cool autumn night. The sky was dark except for the silver glow of a nearly full moon, but white lights had been strung through the bare branches overhead. Then Beatrice saw that the lights were, in fact, hundreds of tiny fairies shimmering in the trees. It was breathtaking, especially when the wind caused the branches to blow and the fairy-lights seemed to flicker like twinkling stars against the black sky.

Amarantha, Gus, and Birdella moved among the guests serving witches' brew. Most Worthy Piddle appeared to be holding court, with Neva and some of the other guests gathered around the chaise lounge on the terrace that he had apparently seized as his throne.

Beatrice reached for a glass from a passing tray as did another guest. Their hands bumped and they both uttered hasty apologies. It was the young woman in navy robes who had nearly fallen asleep over her dinner. "So clumsy of me," she murmured now, and yawned.

"It was as much my fault as yours," Beatrice said. "I wasn't watching. I'm Beatrice Bailey . . . uh . . . wick. Bailiwick."

"Griselda Batty."

Beatrice noticed that the other witch had purple smudges under her eyes and didn't look well.

"Are you feeling all right?" Beatrice asked her.

"Just exhausted," the woman replied. She yawned again. "I'm here on doctor's orders. She says I work too hard. I'm supposed to do nothing but relax for two weeks."

Before Beatrice could reply, a beeping sound emanated from the woman's person.

"My pager," Griselda said, fumbling inside her robes.

Suddenly Neva was there beside them. "No, no, Ms. Batty," she said pleasantly but firmly. "Remember the rules? No laptops, no cell phones, no fax machines, and no pagers."

"Just this one message," Griselda said in a pleading voice. "It might be my mother. My dear, sickly old mother."

Neva's smile never faltered. "Your mother, Ms. Batty, is on a honeymoon cruise with her fourth husband—a warlock named Comus Endor, I believe. Now give me the pager—that's a good witch—and I'll show you up to bed."

Beatrice stared as Neva led Griselda away. "I've never seen so many strange people and critters in one place before," she said.

"It's only just begun," Cyrus informed her. "Look behind you."

Beatrice, Teddy, and Ollie all turned together to look. There was a collective gasp, because standing only a few feet away was a dragon! Its body was covered with coppery scales that glittered in the fairy-light. It had reddish brown wings tucked into its sides, golden claws, and a long tail that could probably knock down the four of them with a single wag.

Once Beatrice had recovered from the shock of seeing a creature that was reputed to kill witches for sport, she noticed that the dragon was surprisingly small—no more than four feet tall. It must be a baby dragon, she decided. And it seemed quite tame as it lapped up witches' brew from a bowl the size of a large cauldron.

Birdella was passing by with a tray of drinks.

"That dragon—" Beatrice began.

"Yes?" Birdella said, as though dragons were a common sight at Skull House.

"What's it *doing* here?"

"He's one of Neva's strays."

"You mean, Neva rescues dragons, too?" Teddy said. "But this is different from a ghost cat or an enchanted donkey. Dragons are dangerous."

"Right," Beatrice said. "They breathe fire and eat people."

Birdella sighed. "Regular dragons do," she said, as if explaining this to four-year-olds. "But Fairarmfull is an Oriental dragon, and they're small and cute and loveable. They don't ever breathe fire except when asked to politely for the purposes of a cookout, and they hardly ever eat people."

"So you're saying this dragon is a pet," Ollie said.

Birdella nodded. "Neva got him from the dragon shelter when he was just four months old. His former owner kept him chained in the backyard and wouldn't even play fetch with him. Poor thing," she added sadly. "You'd think people would know better."

About that time, Amarantha rolled what looked like a bowling ball across the grass and Fairarmfull left his witches' brew to scamper after it. *See?* Birdella's look seemed to say before she left with her tray.

"Enjoying yourselves?" came a man's voice from behind them.

Beatrice and the others turned around and saw that the young couple in hiking clothes had joined them.

"Hello, I'm Roger Middlemarch." The man stuck out his hand like a mortal, and they all shook it. "I'm a senior at Witch U, with a double major in witch history and anthropology." He preened a little before he nodded toward his companion. "This is Matilda Cronk."

"So nice to meet you," Matilda said brightly.

Roger glanced over his shoulder at the crowd around Most Worthy Piddle. "You'd think he'd discovered the cure for witch fever the way everyone fawns and fusses over him," Roger said with a sneer. "But I took his Advanced Spells seminar my junior year, and I wasn't impressed. A lot of the course was just a rehash of Intermediate Spells, and some of the incantations he gave us were blatantly erroneous."

"Not so loud, Roger dear," Matilda whispered. She looked around nervously to see if he had been overheard. "Everyone says that Dr. Piddle is the most learned witch in the sphere. Maybe it's just age catching up with him. He's no spring chicken, after all."

"Don't make excuses," Roger said sharply. "He's presenting himself as a brilliant witch-mind, when, in fact, he's nothing more than—"

"Roger," Matilda said quickly, "I'm sure these young people don't want to hear any more about Dr. Piddle."

"Who does?" Roger wanted to know. "It's time he stepped down and made room for new blood."

Matilda squeezed his arm and looked at him

adoringly. "Why don't you tell them about your project, sweetheart?"

Roger's face lit up. "Oh, yes, it's quite exciting," he said. "I'm here to search for a rare type of brownie that's believed to live in this part of the sphere. There have been occasional sightings for decades, but no one has been able to document the existence of the creature with photos or videotapes."

"How interesting," Beatrice said politely, thinking the opposite. "Are you searching for brownies, too?" she asked Matilda.

"I'm only here as Roger's gofer," Matilda replied. "The search for Higgledy-piggledy Moondust Brownies is his project. It's an honor to play even a small part in such important work."

"And you play that small part so well," Roger said, beaming at her.

"Touching," Teddy muttered.

"If Roger can prove that the Higgledy-piggledy Moondust Brownie does exist, he'll be famous," Matilda said.

"Probably more famous than Dr. Fraud over there," Roger said, scowling in the direction of the witch tutor.

Luckily, the entertainment was beginning and there was no further opportunity to speak with the brownie hunters. The guests even moved away from Most Worthy Piddle to look out over the field, where a band of skeletons called The Rattlebones had assembled and were playing a lively tune called "The Dry Bone Polka."

Ghosts began to float out from behind headstones in

the Bone Yard. Dozens of apparitions came together in the night sky to dance in the moonlight.

"Don't you think it's time to turn in?" Ollie asked Beatrice.

"I suppose so."

But at that moment Most Worthy Piddle walked up to her. He was wearing his gray silk hat with the gold stars and crescent moons. Silver hair covered his shoulders like a fur cape, and dark eyes glittered in his craggy face.

"Forgive me for not introducing myself sooner," he said. His voice was deep and melodious. "I am Most Worthy Piddle."

"I'm Beatrice—"

"Everyone here knows who you are," he said with a dismissive wave of his hand. "You're a distant relation of Bromwich of Bailiwick, one of the most powerful sorcerers who ever lived, and you've come to try to break Dally Rumpe's spell."

Beatrice was at a loss for words. She hadn't expected anyone to know who she was, much less why she was there.

Most Worthy's eyes narrowed as he studied her. "Do you have any idea how dangerous this is? Dally Rumpe will do whatever he must to stop you."

Beatrice felt a prickling of fear. She didn't like the casual way in which he spoke the evil sorcerer's name. She wondered if he knew Dally Rumpe personally.

As though reading her mind, Most Worthy said, "We were acquaintances long ago, Dally Rumpe and I. Of course, I'm sure I wouldn't even recognize him now, he takes on so many different identities." Suddenly he frowned and stared hard into Beatrice's face. "I give you fair warning, Beatrice Bailey—you should leave the Witches' Sphere and go back where you came from. *While you still can.*"

10

The Letter

Beatrice had frightening dreams that night—
or rather, it was the same nightmare over and
over. When the dream began, she was lying in
the dragon bed feeling drowsy and content. Then she
heard footsteps in the hall—the dull thud of heavy boots
against stone, moving slowly and deliberately down the
corridor toward her room.

Beatrice knew that the unknown stalker was searching
for her. A chill ran up her spine. She held her breath,
listening, waiting. The footsteps came closer. Just outside
her door, they stopped.

Beatrice froze. Her heart pounded against her ribs. She
heard the doorknob rattle, then a sliver of light showed
from the torches in the corridor as the door creaked
slowly open.

Something dark and infinitely menacing filled the
doorway before it stepped into the room. With the light to
its back, the intruder was faceless and unidentifiable, but
Beatrice could feel evil emanating from this unwelcome
visitor. It seemed to stare through the darkness until it
found her by some curious type of radar. Then it started
toward her.

A scream formed in Beatrice's throat, but she held it back. She was trying to think—how to get away, how to get past this thing to the door—as the creature approached her bed. Against the light from the hall, Beatrice could see a dark arm rise into the air. The full sleeve of a witch's robes fell back, and Beatrice could make out the silhouette of a hand. Of long bony fingers reaching for her.

Beatrice screamed. The next thing she knew, she was being flung from the bed. She landed in a heap of twisted linens on the cold floor.

That's when Beatrice woke from her nightmarish sleep. She *was* lying on the floor in a tangle of sheets, but it wasn't a monster standing over her. It was Neva.

Beatrice stared at the other witch, who had the sleeves of her robes rolled up and was wearing a bibbed apron. Beatrice watched, not comprehending at first, as Neva mumbled and pointed at the bedding that was wound around Beatrice's body. The sheets immediately unwound themselves and floated to the bed, where they pulled themselves taut and tucked their edges neatly under the mattress. The quilted coverlet rose from the floor, spread itself out in midair, and settled lightly over the bed.

"You zapped me out of bed!" Beatrice exclaimed.

"There's work to be done—floors to be swept and beds to be made," Neva said cheerfully. "You know what they say, my dear—the early witch catches the goblin."

"I've never heard that saying," Beatrice grumbled.

From under the covers in the griffin bed, Teddy giggled.

Beatrice and Teddy got dressed and went to collect the boys for breakfast. The foursome and Cayenne had just entered the dining room when they heard loud voices from the kitchen.

Beatrice exchanged a look with her friends. "I guess we might as well," she said, and pushed open the kitchen door.

Neva was standing in the middle of the room with her hands on her ample hips. Birdella was on her hands and knees, scrubbing the floor vigorously with a soapy sponge. All across the tiles were dark spots that looked like tiny chocolate-pudding footprints. The entire kitchen was in disarray. A bottle of milk had been spilled on the counter, a half-eaten cake and a trail of crumbs littered the table, apple cores and orange rinds had been flung into every corner, and jelly handprints no bigger than Beatrice's pinky nail covered everything from the refrigerator to the bread box.

"What happened?" Beatrice and her friends all asked at once.

"Frisk happened." Neva looked around in disgust.

"Is Frisk another stray?" Beatrice asked sympathetically.

"Good grief, no!" Neva responded. "Frisk is an elf."

"He's not related to *my* family," Birdella said quickly, looking up from her scrubbing. "Though I think he might be a distant cousin of Gus's."

"He lives in the cellar," Neva said, "which is fine—I never even asked him to pay rent—and he comes up every night after we're asleep to eat me out of house and home. I could live with that, as well. What I *can't* live with are his slovenly, harum-scarum, willy-nilly ways!"

"Can't you evict him?" Cyrus asked.

"It isn't that easy," Neva said tartly. "I've asked him to leave and he refuses. We'll have to trap him. But it takes a special trap to catch an elf. Tricky work."

"It's wise to hire a professional," Birdella added.

"Hammet the Elf Man is the best around," Neva said, "but he's backed up until Candlemas."

"Hammet doesn't do anything—*harmful* to the elves, does he?" Ollie asked.

"Certainly not!" Neva looked shocked and offended. "He gives them a choice of several locales—nice communities where elves have lived for centuries—and provides first-class travel accommodations. That's one reason elf-catchers are paid so well."

When Beatrice and her friends left the kitchen, Roger Middlemarch waved them over to the table where he and Matilda were sitting. Beatrice went reluctantly, followed by the others.

"Merry meet," Roger said. "Did you sleep well?" he asked solicitously.

They all said good morning, and yes, they had slept very well, thank you.

"We heard a rumor," Roger said, lowering his voice, "that there was a small intruder in the kitchen last night. Is it true?"

"An elf from the cellar," Teddy said.

Roger looked disappointed. "Are you sure? It takes an expert to differentiate between the tracks of an elf and those of a brownie."

"Neva seemed quite certain," Beatrice said. "I believe she knows this particular elf personally."

"Oh." Roger's face drooped further. "Then I'll just have to keep looking for my elusive brownies."

"You'll find them," Matilda assured him.

"How rude of me to keep you standing," Roger said suddenly. "Won't you all join us?"

"I don't think there's room," Beatrice said quickly. "Maybe we can talk after breakfast."

"Fine," Roger said. "You might be interested in seeing some brownie drawings I have. They're reproductions of sketches made by an artist who actually saw the brownies."

How interesting, love to, Beatrice and her friends murmured, and edged away.

Amarantha seated them near Most Worthy Piddle's table. This morning the witch tutor was wearing forest green robes and a matching silk hat that had a gold dragon embroidered around the pointed crown.

"He must spend a fortune on his clothes," Teddy whispered.

They ordered serpent's eggs—sunny-side up—toast with catmint jelly, and moonbeam tea. Beatrice looked up several times during the meal to see Dr. Piddle staring at her.

"That man makes me nervous," she said under her breath. "I don't care if he *is* the greatest witch scholar that ever lived."

"You're sounding like Roger now." Teddy grinned.

"You should compare notes when he shows you his brownie sketches."

"I'll be the first to admit that Roger's a bore," Beatrice whispered, "but that doesn't mean he's stupid. Maybe he *has* picked up on something about Most Worthy that everyone else has missed."

"Dr. Piddle does seem unusually interested in you, Beatrice," Ollie said.

"He probably wants to be Beatrice's tutor," Teddy said in a sassy voice. "After she breaks Dally Rumpe's spell and becomes a Classical witch, I mean."

"Don't even joke about it," Beatrice muttered. "At the very least, he's obnoxious."

"And at most, he's what?" Ollie asked.

Beatrice shrugged. "A fraud, I guess. Isn't that what Roger called him?"

Just then, Neva came into the dining room looking flushed and excited. "May I have your attention, please?" she said in her booming voice. "Your attention, please."

Everyone stopped talking.

"After breakfast," Neva said, "we're offering our guests a special treat—a day trip to the largest haunted theme park in the Witches' Sphere."

"Seven Screams!" Cyrus shouted.

Neva beamed at Cyrus. "That's right, young man. Vehicles will be lining up out front in a few minutes to take you to Seven Screams."

Teddy said, "Oh, we have to go. I've heard about Seven Screams all my life."

"I've read that it's the best amusement park ever," Ollie agreed.

Teddy, Cyrus, and Ollie began sharing every wonderful thing they had heard about the theme park. Finally, Teddy noticed that Beatrice hadn't said a word.

"Aren't you excited about going to Seven Screams?" she asked Beatrice.

"I am," Beatrice said. "But what about our instructions from the Witches' Executive Committee? Someone should be here when they come."

"Oh, yeah," Teddy said. She and the boys looked dejected.

"We should all be here," Ollie said. "Sorry, Beatrice, I was forgetting why we came. This isn't a vacation."

"That's right, we'll all stay," Cyrus said, but his disappointment was obvious.

Beatrice thought about it, and then she said, "The instructions may not even come today, and if they do, I could ask Neva to send you a message."

Teddy perked up. "Do you think that would be all right?"

"Let me see if Neva could get you back quickly."

Neva assured Beatrice that her friends could be brought back to Skull House in ten minutes, if need be.

"Then it's settled," Beatrice said. "You guys go and have a great time."

Teddy was glum again. "I'd feel too guilty," she said.

"Yeah, we can't go without you," Cyrus agreed.

"Yes, you can," Beatrice said firmly. "I really don't mind. Roller coasters terrify me and the spinning rides make me sick. So go and have fun and don't give me another thought."

Beatrice went outside with her friends to bid them

good-bye, and was astonished to see three magic carpets floating in midair in front of Skull House.

"Can you *believe* this?" Teddy started dancing around in delight.

"Just don't do that once we're on the rug," Cyrus warned, but he was looking pretty excited himself.

"Are you sure you won't change your mind?" Ollie asked Beatrice. "How many chances do you get to ride on one of these things?"

"You can tell me about it," Beatrice said. "And don't forget to bring back lots of junk food."

"You got it," Ollie promised.

He climbed up on the first carpet with Teddy and Cyrus. Griselda Batty was on the next one with Amarantha and Crispin the donkey. Beatrice was relieved to see Roger Middlemarch and Matilda Cronk board the third carpet with Wooly Mittens. *Thank goodness*, Beatrice thought. She wouldn't have to look at brownie sketches after all.

Roger and Matilda were waving to her as the carpets took off. "We'll catch you later," Roger called.

The magic carpets soared into the air, and Beatrice waved until they were out of sight. Then she and Cayenne went back inside.

What to do all day, she wondered, while her friends were off having the time of their lives? "I think I'll read," she said to Cayenne.

"The library's through that door."

Beatrice jumped. She had thought she was alone in the lobby, but there was Gus pointing to a door at the end of the front desk.

"Uh—thank you," Beatrice said.

Gus scowled. "My pleasure," he muttered, and stomped out of the room.

"Such a loveable guy," Beatrice said under her breath. "Hello, Tom," she added to the two glowing eyes under the stairs.

Floor-to-ceiling bookshelves lined the walls of the library. The room smelled of old paper and dust and mold. Cayenne sneezed, then leaped into a wingback chair to take a nap while Beatrice searched the shelves for interesting titles.

Amid the rows of dark unattractive bindings, one volume caught Beatrice's eye. It was beautifully bound in rich red leather. Beatrice reached for the book instinctively, wondering why there was no title on the spine, and was further puzzled to see that the front cover was blank, as well. She opened the book and was disappointed to find that the pages were also blank. *Just an old journal*, Beatrice thought, and was replacing it on the shelf when the book seemed to wrest itself from her hands and fall to the floor.

Beatrice cried out in alarm, startling Cayenne awake. The cat and her mistress watched as the pages of the book began to turn of their own accord, and then stop just as suddenly—at a page where words the color of fresh blood had been scrawled. Beatrice's heart was galloping as she forced herself to lean closer to read the words.

"*I am watching you, Beatrice Bailey*," she read in a strained voice. "*Go home now! Time is running out.*"

Cayenne's luminous eyes narrowed. She uttered a soft meow and leaped to Beatrice's shoulder. Beatrice had been staring at the crude message as if bewitched, unable to tear her eyes away until Cayenne jolted her out of her trance. Now she took a deep breath, and muttered, "Watch me all you like," before kicking the loathsome book to the other side of the library.

Cayenne nestled against Beatrice's hair and responded with a gritty purr to signify her approval.

Beatrice would have liked nothing better than to get out of there, but she forced herself to stay until she found some books to read. She was feeling almost calm—and a little proud of herself—when she emerged into the lobby a few minutes later.

She had selected four books: *A Tale of Two Witches; The Witches' Sphere on a Shoestring; Dragons, Dragons Everywhere;* and *Gone with the Witch.* Conscious that someone might be watching her at that very moment, Beatrice resisted the urge to look back over her shoulder or give any sign that the incident in the library had frightened her. She went out to the terrace with her books and settled into a lounge chair to read. Cayenne stretched out in the sun at her feet.

Neva was raking leaves. In actual fact, she was pointing at a rake and the rake was speeding across the lawn on its own, leaving tidy piles of leaves in its wake.

Beatrice blew her bangs out of her eyes and opened *Dragons, Dragons Everywhere.* The author claimed that there had once been a dragon on every street corner, in every village, on every farm. To hear him tell it, dragons were as commonplace as field mice. And so were brush fires. The text wasn't especially interesting, but Beatrice loved the color prints of dragons through the ages.

While she was looking at the pictures, Beatrice became aware of warm breath on the back of her neck. At first she thought Cayenne had climbed up behind her, but then she looked down and saw the cat asleep at her feet. Beatrice's body tensed. She spun around—and found herself staring into the glittering red eyes of Fairarmfull the dragon.

Beatrice's heart lurched. First a warning written in blood, now a dragon. She didn't care if he was Neva's pet, Beatrice found the presence of this creature disconcerting. Then she realized that Fairarmfull was looking at a print in the book, apparently so captivated by the picture of a dragon breathing fire on a knight that he wasn't aware of Beatrice at all.

Beatrice exhaled slowly. She looked at the print, then back at Fairarmfull. "Don't even think about it," she said.

After a while, the little dragon lost interest in the pictures. He wandered off and began to nudge the bowling ball around the yard with his nose.

"Isn't that cute?" Birdella said. She had brought out a basketful of laundry to hang on the line. The elf chanted brightly:

> Socks and trousers,
> Sheets and hose,
> Line up smartly
> In double rows.

Wet clothing and bed linens promptly leaped from the basket and grabbed hold of one of the two clotheslines that stretched across the yard.

With so many gone to Seven Screams, the dining room was nearly empty at lunchtime. A couple of local witches stopped in for the day's special, oregano cheese pie and pears in caterpillar sauce, and a man Beatrice had never seen before was sitting alone at a back table. She noticed that his edges were a little blurred, but he seemed too solid to be a ghost.

When Birdella came to the table with a menu, Beatrice asked, "Is that man a ghost?"

The elf nodded, her tight-lipped expression suggesting that she didn't like him very much.

"Then why isn't he more—wispy?"

"Ghosts reflect what they were in life," Birdella said. "This one was hard and demanding—*anything* but wispy." She sighed, and added grimly, "I'd better go serve him before he starts making a fuss."

The man was reading a book and didn't look very friendly, Beatrice observed as she watched him over the top of her menu. His white hair fell from a center part to just past his ears. He was wearing an old-fashioned black coat and a gold brocade vest. A top hat and a silver-tipped cane rested on the chair beside him.

Beatrice heard Birdella say, "What can I bring you, sir?"

The ghost looked up from his book and replied, "Since I can't actually *eat* anything, I'll have to settle for something that *smells* delicious. What would you recommend?"

"Uh . . . well . . . let's see . . . uh . . . something that smells delicious—" Birdella was caught off guard and could do little more than stammer as she tried to come up with a suggestion.

"Confound it, you little elf," the ghost said sharply. "You're a waitress, aren't you? Can't you at least recommend something fragrant for my lunch?"

Birdella looked like she might start crying. "I'm sorry, sir," she managed to say. "Uh—"

"I think," came a deep voice from behind Beatrice, "that frog's liver and onions might do the trick. *Very* aromatic."

Beatrice turned to look at the speaker. Yes, just as she had thought, it was Most Worthy Piddle. He struck a pose in the doorway, then made a grand entrance, attired in yet another set of robes and hat. This outfit was royal blue, the hat adorned with silver pentagrams. Teddy would be sorry she missed it, Beatrice mused.

The witch tutor came over to Beatrice's table and said, "Would you mind very much if I joined you, Ms. Bailey?"

Too polite to respond truthfully, Beatrice said, "Of course not."

"I believe I *will* have the frog's liver," the ghost said to Birdella. Then he bestowed upon Dr. Piddle a grimace that was, no doubt, supposed to be a smile. "Thank you for the suggestion, Most Worthy."

"My pleasure, Algernon," the witch tutor replied as he sat down across from Beatrice. "An old acquaintance of mine," he said softly. "When you get to be my age, it seems you know everyone. *That* rude fellow is a ghost writer by the name of Algernon Puffin. Not much of a writer, actually. He has an entertainment column and does book reviews for *The Specter*."

At Beatrice's blank look, Most Worthy Piddle added, "A weekly newspaper for ghosts, but everyone in the sphere reads it. Algernon claims to be working on a blockbuster novel, which we've been hearing about for at least eighty years. He fancies himself to be a sort of disembodied Hemingway." The witch tutor laughed unpleasantly. Then he said, "Have you ordered, my dear? Then may I recommend the oregano cheese pie? It really is excellent."

When Birdella came back to the table, Dr. Piddle ordered for both of them. Which was fine with Beatrice, since the faster they were served, the sooner she could get away from the man. Cayenne didn't seem to like him, either. She climbed into Beatrice's lap and sat very still, staring at the witch tutor with her round knowing eyes.

"I'm glad for the opportunity to speak privately," Most Worthy said after Birdella had brought their meals. His dark eyes never left Beatrice's face. "Now about this plan to break Dally Rumpe's spell and free Bromwich. I'm sure you feel a responsibility to try, his being a relation of yours."

"That's right," Beatrice said. She lowered her eyes and concentrated on her food to avoid the man's piercing stare.

"And then there's the matter of your classification," the witch tutor continued. "I imagine you were flattered when Thaddeus Thigpin and Aura Featherstone showed up and offered to test you."

Beatrice made a noncommittal sound. She could hear the amusement in his voice, and knew that he was mocking her. *A lowly Reform witch*, he must be thinking, *having the audacity to believe that she stands a chance against a sorcerer as powerful as Dally Rumpe!*

"My advice to you, Beatrice Bailey, is *don't do it!*"

Beatrice looked up at him. His expression was cold, perhaps even cruel. The man frightened her.

She took time to collect herself. Then she said quietly, "My name is Bailiwick. Beatrice Bailiwick."

Most Worthy Piddle's mouth twisted into a sneer. "As you wish, Ms. *Bailiwick.* Just remember that I tried to warn you."

"It isn't likely that I'll forget," Beatrice said.

The witch tutor was opening his mouth to speak again when Algernon Puffin let out a roar. Beatrice flinched, and even Most Worthy Piddle twisted around in his chair to scowl at the ghost writer.

"What the—"

"Unbelievable!" Algernon Puffin screeched. His face was scarlet and he looked very angry. He saw Beatrice watching him, and he said, "Young woman—yes, *you.* How many young women do you see at your table? Tell me, are you a witch?"

"Yes," Beatrice said, wondering what she was letting herself in for.

"Then tell me, as a witch," the ghost writer said, holding up a book and shaking it, "what you think of an author—a *mortal* author," he added, his lips curling in distaste, "who claims to be an expert on witches, and uses the term *warlock* for a male witch!"

"I think," Beatrice said slowly, "that the author is ill informed."

The ghost stared at her. "Ill informed," he muttered. "*Ill informed*, you say? Well, aren't you the tactful and well-mannered one?" he screamed.

Beatrice glared at the ghost. "Things you obviously know nothing about," she snapped.

But Algernon Puffin had already forgotten about her. He was ranting and raging to himself, and banging the book on the table. "Any *imbecile* knows that a witch is a witch—be the witch a he or a she! To call a male witch a warlock—an oath breaker!—is an insult. It's an outrage!"

Then suddenly, there were *two* Algernon Puffins sitting there. And each one was banging a book on the table. "I'm just so angry, I'm beside myself! Simply *beside myself!*" he shrieked.

The ghost writer's tantrum gave Beatrice a headache. She was grateful when lunch was finished and she could retreat with Cayenne and her books to the terrace.

It was late that afternoon when Beatrice saw a large black bird land in the yard. On its back was a little man dressed all in brown. He slid off the bird's back and headed toward Beatrice.

"Registered mail delivery for Beatrice Bailiwick," he said in a bored tone. "Are you Beatrice Bailiwick?"

Beatrice felt a rush of excitement mixed with dread. "Yes . . . that is . . . I'm called Bailey now—but Bailiwick *was* my name—well, I guess it still is, officially—"

"Sign here." He interrupted her nervous babbling by shoving a clipboard and pen beneath her nose.

Beatrice had barely finished writing a B when the pen took over. *Which is a good thing*, she thought, because her hand was trembling so badly, her own signature would have been illegible.

When Beatrice was anxious, she tended to talk too much, and so she said now, "Is that a raven you're riding?"

"Crow," the man said curtly. From the look on his face, Beatrice concluded that a crow must be on the low end of the air transportation scale.

"So that's how mail is delivered here."

"*Registered* mail," he snapped. "The rest is delivered using ground transport—jackrabbits for cross-sphere, frogs for local."

Beatrice took a good hard look at the man. "Are you by any chance a brownie?" she asked.

He touched the front of his brown tunic and frowned. "What *else* would I be?" he asked sarcastically.

"Well, it's just that I've never met a brownie," Beatrice said. "In fact, it's been a long time since I've even read about one—"

"Don't rub it in!" The brownie's lips drew together in a pout. "It's the witches who get all the press these days. No one gives a thought to brownies anymore."

He thrust an envelope into Beatrice's hand and stalked back to his crow.

"Are you a Higgledy-piggledy Moondust Brownie?" Beatrice called after him.

He came to an abrupt stop and pivoted around. "Another one of those ridiculous myths!" he shouted. "For the last time, there's *no such thing* as a Higgledy-piggledy Moondust Brownie!"

He climbed onto the crow's back and took off without so much as a "good day."

Beatrice didn't take time to dwell on her meeting with the brownie. She had a cream-colored envelope in her hand addressed to Beatrice Bailiwick. The return address read: Witches' Institute, Executive Committee, Suite #7, 13 Talisman Lane, Witches' Sphere.

Beatrice tore open the envelope. Inside, she found a letter and a copy of the Bailiwick map. A path of minuscule footprints had been drawn on the map in silver ink. The path led through forests and fields from Skull House to Winter Wood.

Beatrice put the map aside and focused on the letter. It read:

Dear Ms. Bailiwick,

The Executive Committee of the Witches' Institute requests that you and your party leave for Winter Wood tomorrow morning after you have availed yourselves of a nutritious breakfast. You should take with you a warm coat, hat, and gloves. Enclosed you will find a map that shows the quickest and safest route to Winter Wood. Do not stray from this path!

On behalf of the entire committee, I wish you all the best in your Noble Quest.

Sincerely,

Thaddeus Q. Thigpin
Director, Witches' Institute

Beatrice read the letter a second time. It said so little! She had expected detailed instructions—maybe even some helpful spells. All the committee had sent was a map. And Thaddeus Q. Thigpin's best wishes.

11

The Silver Path

Beatrice was in the lobby playing Clue with Neva and Birdella when the magic carpets returned from Seven Screams. Most Worthy Piddle and Algernon Puffin sat nearby arguing over a game of chess. Beatrice heard the carpets squeal to a stop, and then Gus appeared out of nowhere to open the door.

Amarantha and Griselda Batty came in first, looking tired and windblown and happy. Roger Middlemarch and Matilda Cronk came next. His face was an alarming shade of green.

Matilda smiled and waved at Beatrice. "He's sick, poor baby—from eating three hexburgers and a bag of caramel charms before riding the roller coaster. So no wonder! Sit down, Roger, and I'll ask Neva if she has something to soothe your stomach."

Wooly Mittens ran in looking fit as a fiddle, and Cayenne dashed over to greet him. Crispin followed, wearing an orange baseball cap with *Seven Screams* printed on it in black. Beatrice's friends were last. Their cheeks were pink and they were giggling. Even Ollie.

"I can see you had a great time," Beatrice said.

"Oh, Beatrice, it was so much fun!" Teddy exclaimed. "I wish you had come."

"They have the biggest roller coaster I've ever seen," Cyrus told her. "It's called The Avenger."

"And great junk food," Ollie said.

"Speaking of food . . ." Teddy handed Beatrice an orange bag. "A devil dog with ketchup, mustard, and onions, and a giant-size serving of fury fries. But take it easy with the fries—they'll burn your mouth."

"And here's dessert," Ollie added, handing her another bag. "Jelly jinxes and marshmallow monsters and banshee brittle."

"I love the jelly jinxes," Cyrus said. He frowned and patted his belly. "Maybe I overdid it a little."

"Well, you'd better recover fast," Beatrice said. She couldn't keep the news to herself another second. "The letter came. We leave for Winter Wood in the morning."

Her friends just stared at her, not at all the response Beatrice had expected. Then Teddy said in a subdued voice, "So it's really happening."

"What does the letter say?" Ollie asked, appearing equally solemn.

"Not much," Beatrice said. "Just that we're to leave in the morning and take warm clothing with us. And there's a map that shows us how to get there. Let's go upstairs and you can see it."

Just then Neva waved her hands to get their attention. "I know some of you aren't feeling well after your outing to

Seven Screams," she said kindly, "so I have a soothing brew waiting in the dining room. It's very tasty—even if you're feeling quite well, I think you'll enjoy a cup before bed."

"I'd better have some of that," Cyrus said weakly.

"Let's all have a cup," Beatrice suggested. "Then I'll show you the map and the letter."

Everyone crowded into the dining room, where Amarantha was pouring a steaming liquid into mugs.

Ollie took a sip and smiled. "It's good. Like hot chocolate, only better."

"No, it has a strawberry flavor," Teddy said.

Cyrus shook his head. "Uh-uh, definitely caramel."

"You're all wrong," Beatrice said. "It tastes like coconut cream pie."

Most Worthy Piddle was standing beside her with a mug in his hands. "It's called Personal Taste Brew," he said, squinting at Beatrice through the steam rising in front of his face. "Each of us has a favorite sweet, and that's what the brew will taste like to us. This drink tastes just like creamy butterscotch to me."

"It *smells* like lemon meringue pie." Algernon Puffin had stuck his head into the steam from Most Worthy's mug and was sniffing noisily.

"Stop that," the witch tutor said sharply. "Honestly, Algernon, you've picked up some disgusting habits since you died."

Much to Beatrice's relief, the witch and the ghost began to bicker, which allowed her to move away without them noticing.

"I feel a lot better," Cyrus announced after his second cup of brew.

"Then let's go look at the letter and the map," Ollie said.

They headed for Beatrice and Teddy's room, where Beatrice withdrew the letter from Cayenne's pocket in the backpack. The others gathered around as Beatrice pulled the letter and map from the envelope.

"That's strange," Beatrice said. "I distinctly remember placing the letter on top of the map. But now the map's on top."

"Are you sure that's how you left them?" Teddy asked.

"Positive."

"Then somebody else must have looked in the envelope," Ollie said.

Beatrice was worried. After reading that frightening message in the library, she could only assume that Dally Rumpe was observing their every move. "Someone could have been watching when the letter was delivered," she said. "He—or she—had most of the afternoon to sneak in here and read it."

"So who didn't go to Seven Screams?" Teddy asked.

"Most Worthy Piddle didn't go," Beatrice said promptly. "I don't trust him at all, and he's tried awfully hard to get me to go home."

"What's the name of the guy who was arguing with Most Worthy?" Cyrus asked.

"Algernon Puffin," Beatrice replied, "the ghost writer."

"Well, he isn't very likeable," Cyrus said, "and he didn't go with us."

"Neither did Gus," Teddy said. "Don't you all think he's peculiar? And Birdella didn't go, either. But she's so nice."

"Maybe *too* nice," Cyrus said darkly. "What about Neva? She was here all day."

"Yeah, but Neva wouldn't read Beatrice's private mail," Teddy protested.

"How can you be sure?" Ollie asked her. "We don't really know Neva, do we? We don't know anyone here very well. Hey—I just thought of something. Someone could have looked at the letter after we got back from Seven Screams. We were downstairs for quite a while."

"That's right," Beatrice said. "And dumb me—we were in the lobby with everyone standing around when I told you the letter had come. Anyone could have heard me."

"And then sneaked up here while we were in the dining room drinking Personal Taste Brew," Cyrus concluded.

"Who all was in the dining room?" Teddy asked. "I know I saw Algernon Puffin and Most Worthy Piddle. And Gus and Birdella and Neva."

"I remember Roger and Matilda," Cyrus said. "And Crispin. And Amarantha."

"But were all of them there the whole time?" Ollie asked.

"I wasn't paying much attention," Teddy admitted.

"Well, there's nothing we can do now," Ollie said, "so let's stop thinking about it."

In spite of his reassuring calm, Beatrice could see that Ollie was every bit as worried as she was.

That night, Beatrice dreamed about the faceless intruder again. As before, she heard heavy footsteps in the hall that stopped just outside her room. Then the door opened with a groan. The creature started across the room toward her, but this time Beatrice woke up before it reached her. She sat up in the dragon bed and peered around the dark room to assure herself that no one was lurking in the shadows. Then Teddy startled her by crying out in her sleep.

"It's okay, Teddy—nothing but a bad dream."

Her words seemed to calm Teddy, but Beatrice couldn't go back to sleep. She huddled in bed under the quilted coverlet until she saw the first hint of pink light on the horizon. Then she got up and took a long hot shower.

Dressed in jeans and comfortable shoes, Beatrice and her companions brought their backpacks with them to breakfast. They had scarcely sat down when Amarantha arrived with heaping plates of food.

"Wooly Mittens ordered big breakfasts for you—basically, everything on the menu," Amarantha said. "You'll need strength for your journey."

Beatrice looked at her sharply. "How did Wooly Mittens know that we're going on a journey?"

Amarantha looked surprised at the question. "You can't keep a secret at Skull House," she said, and left.

They stuffed themselves with serpents' eggs, brimstone biscuits with melted butter and catmint jelly, and hot cereal with honey and dragon's milk. Beatrice felt that every eye in the room was on them while they ate. She wondered if any of those eyes belonged to Dally Rumpe.

Beatrice looked around at the other diners. There was Algernon Puffin, holding up a book and appearing to read, but Beatrice stared at him for a long time and he never turned a page. At another table was Most Worthy Piddle, resplendent this morning in white robes with a gold unicorn on his hat. Most Worthy had made no secret of his opposition to Beatrice's Quest, and his dark eyes were boring into her now. Was he the great witch he professed to be or a fraud?

Then there was Roger—tedious Roger, who might or might not really be at Skull House in search of a rare brownie, which might or might not actually exist. And Beatrice couldn't forget Roger's gofer and girlfriend, Matilda Cronk, who was either the most devoted companion who ever lived or a world-class actress. And next to the brownie hunters was Crispin the donkey, who appeared to have no interest in anything at the moment except his sage oatcakes—but obviously, things might not be as they seemed with a donkey who wasn't a donkey at all.

Anyone at Skull House could be my enemy, Beatrice thought. Crabby, curmudgeonly Gus, for instance. He was always lurking around, watching and listening and turning up in unexpected places. And what about Birdella? Her work took her to every part of Skull House and gave her ample opportunity to snoop in the guests' rooms. And there was Amarantha, who seemed to know entirely too much about them and where they were going. Ollie was right, Beatrice concluded, they couldn't eliminate anyone from the list of suspects. Not even their attentive host Wooly Mittens. *So what if Cayenne likes him?* Beatrice thought. What better disguise than to pretend to be a cat? And, of course, Neva had access to all the rooms, not to mention the strong personality one would expect of a powerful sorcerer.

After breakfast, Neva met Beatrice and her friends in the lobby. She gave them bags of sandwiches and fruit for lunch, just as Beatrice's mother had done. Beatrice felt a pang of guilt for suspecting Neva of evil intentions. Birdella was there, too, fussing over them and asking if they had remembered to pack warm hats. Not only did everyone know they were going on a journey, Beatrice reflected, but they apparently knew the destination, as well.

Beatrice was considering this when she noticed movement under the stairs. Then—to her complete surprise—a handsome little ghost-cat crept silently into the light.

"Why, it's Tom," Neva said in surprise. "He's never shown himself to guests before."

Trembling Tom looked around apprehensively, his transparent body quivering, his eyes huge and round. He took a hesitant step toward Cayenne, who moved graciously to meet him.

"He's wishing your cat well," Neva said.

"Thanks, Tom," Beatrice said. "We'll take good care of Cayenne."

"And of yourselves," Neva said briskly. Not one for sentimental farewells, she added, "Try not to do anything stupid."

The air was crisp and the sun was bright as they stepped out into the October morning. *It's a beautiful day to start off on an adventure*, Beatrice thought, and suddenly she felt a surge of exhilaration. For the moment, she forgot to be afraid.

They were headed down the walk toward the road when Ollie exclaimed, "Look at the ground!"

The others looked, and what they saw were a half-dozen silver footprints on the flagstones in front of them.

"It's just like the silver path on the map," Beatrice said in delight.

She stepped forward and another footprint appeared. The path continued to lead them to the road, where it turned north.

"This is so cool," Cyrus said, grinning as he raced after the next footprint. The other three had to quicken their pace to keep up with him.

They followed the footprints up the road for several miles, until the path veered off into a meadow. After a while, large trees began to appear, and the silver path led them into a dense forest. It was dark within the trees, but the footprints glowed like lanterns to show them the way.

The path meandered through the woods, seeming at times to have no logic in its direction. But then Beatrice began to notice that they were always led away from brambles and thick undergrowth. As Dr. Thigpin had written in his letter, the path seemed to be guiding them along the safest route to Winter Wood.

Finally, the trees began to thin out. Beatrice was tired and hungry. She looked up and saw that the sun was directly overhead.

"Let's stop here and have lunch," she said.

The others agreed, and collapsed gratefully into the soft grass that grew alongside a stream.

Beatrice began to hand out the food.

"*Yuck!*" Teddy grimaced as she unwrapped her sandwich. "I can't stand frog's liver. Does anyone want to trade?"

"I will," Cyrus said. "I have serpent's-egg salad."

"No, thanks," Teddy replied. "What do you guys have?"

"Peanut butter and catmint jelly," Ollie said.

Beatrice lifted the top slice of bread on her sandwich. "Frog's liver."

Teddy traded with Ollie.

Beatrice fed Cayenne the salmon that Neva had packed for the cat, then pulled the map out of her backpack.

"How much farther?" Teddy asked.

"I think we've just come through these woods," Beatrice said, pointing out a spot on the map. "If so, we're nearly halfway there."

"We'd better get going," Ollie said. "We don't want to travel at night."

As the day wore on, the landscape became more desolate and forbidding. Fields and forests gave way to barren hills. By late afternoon, they found themselves following the silver footprints up the steep rocky side of a mountain. It wasn't an easy climb, and their progress was slow.

Beatrice stopped to catch her breath. She blew her bangs aside and peered around her. There was nothing to see for miles except more jagged cliffs. It was a sobering sight.

"The sun's going down," Beatrice said. She spoke calmly, trying to ignore the knot of anxiety in her stomach. Then she glanced at her friends' faces and saw her own fears reflected there.

"What do we do now?" Teddy asked.

"Find a place to spend the night," Beatrice said promptly, feigning a confidence that she didn't feel.

"Like *where?*" Cyrus demanded.

Beatrice looked in all directions again, thinking that maybe there was a cave they had overlooked. That's when she saw the little house. It was perched on a flat ledge of rock just a few hundred feet away. Beatrice was so relieved, she laughed out loud, startling the other three.

"*There!*" Beatrice said, pointing toward the house.

Actually, it was no more than a hovel, she realized now, very small and in a sad state of disrepair. It looked like pictures she had seen of a shepherd's hut. But it had a roof and a sturdy door. They would be safe there for the night. Beatrice couldn't have been happier if they had stumbled upon a Holiday Inn, but one thing puzzled her: How could she have missed seeing it before?

"Hot dog," Cyrus said, and started after Beatrice toward the hut.

Beatrice pushed the door open. It was just the one room, with many years' accumulation of dirt and cobwebs. The only furnishings were a crude table, two benches, and piles of straw bedding.

Beatrice looked at her friends and shrugged. "It's better than sleeping outside," she said.

She turned back to the hut—and was astonished by what she saw. The cobwebs had disappeared; in fact, it looked as though the place had been scrubbed clean. Candles burned, giving the room a cozy warmth, and on the table were plates and cups and silverware. And food.

Beatrice couldn't believe what she was seeing. She walked over to the table. There was a large pitcher of—

Beatrice looked inside and decided that it was probably dragon's milk. The ironstone pitcher was cold to the touch, and the milk smelled fresh. There were also two loaves of bread—already buttered and still warm—a wedge of hard cheese, and a bowl filled with ripe peaches.

"*Wow!*" Teddy stopped short in the doorway.

"Who could have done this?" Cyrus asked, staring in amazement at the meal on the table.

"Peregrine, maybe?" Beatrice guessed wildly. "The Witches' Executive Committee?"

"I'll bet it was Neva," Teddy said.

"Or Dally Rumpe," Ollie said with a frown.

"I hadn't thought of that!" Teddy exclaimed. "The food might be poisoned."

"The whole place could be under an evil spell," Cyrus said.

"It's certainly possible," Beatrice agreed. She leaned over to sniff the milk again. Then she broke off a tiny piece of bread and lifted it to her lips.

"Beatrice, don't do it," Teddy warned.

Beatrice allowed the bread to roll around in her mouth, then swallowed. "It tastes okay," she said. "In fact, it's delicious."

The others looked nervously at one another. Meanwhile, Cayenne jumped up on the table and began to nibble on a corner of the cheese. Beatrice pulled her away. But when a few minutes had passed and neither Beatrice nor her familiar had collapsed or turned into a toad, they gave in to their rumbling bellies and sat down to enjoy a good meal.

12

A Hedge of Thorns

eatrice stretched lazily, feeling Cayenne's warm body against her side and forgetting where she was until she opened her eyes and saw beams of sunlight coming through holes in the thatched roof. She rolled over and saw that Teddy and Cyrus were just waking up, the straw beneath them rustling as they came alive. Ollie was still asleep, with one hand knotted into a fist and pressed into his cheek. When Beatrice saw this, she grinned sleepily, picked up a handful of straw and released it over Ollie's head.

As the straw rained down, Ollie started yelling. "What? Ooooooh—I'm drowning! Can't breathe. Can't—"

His arms and legs flailing, Ollie's eyes popped open and he jerked awake. When he realized where he was, and saw his friends' laughing faces, he threw a shoe at them and muttered something under his breath.

"Rise and shine, sleepyhead," Beatrice said with exaggerated cheerfulness. "We have more adventures in store today."

Ollie groaned and squeezed his eyes shut.

"This isn't the most comfortable bed in the world," Cyrus said through a yawn, "but I sure slept like it was."

"Yeah," Teddy said, "I didn't wake up once all night."

"It was as if I'd been enchanted," Beatrice added.

At the mention of enchantment, they all turned silent.

Ollie sat up, frowned at them, and began to pick bits of straw out of his hair. "Is there any food left? I'm starving."

"Me, too," Beatrice said, and jumped up to see about breakfast.

They ate the last of the bread and cheese and packed the remaining peaches to take with them. Eager to be on their way again, they found the path of silver footprints and set off across the cliff.

Before long, the path turned downward. Soon the rocky crags gave way to rolling hills, and then to meadowland.

"It's a lot easier walking on flat ground," Teddy said. "How much farther, do you think?"

Beatrice looked at the map, then peered at a grassy rise up ahead. "I believe Winter Wood is just beyond that hill."

Cyrus gave a nervous laugh. "This is going to sound weird considering how far we've come—but I'm beginning to think this wasn't such a good idea."

"I was just wondering myself what I'm doing here," Beatrice said. "I still don't care about being a Classical witch."

"It's too late now," Teddy responded.

"No it isn't," Ollie said. He looked at Beatrice, and added gently, "We can still turn back—and just call this trip to the Witches' Sphere an interesting Fall Break vacation."

"Ollie, Beatrice has an obligation to Bromwich and his daughters," Teddy said sharply. "She's their only hope."

"Don't worry about piling on the pressure," Beatrice muttered.

"Teddy, you don't care about Beatrice's family obligation," Cyrus said in exasperation. "You just want your chance to be reclassified."

"You make it sound like I'm completely self-centered!" Teddy shouted. "I *resent* that, Cyrus Rascallion."

"You *are* self-centered," Cyrus said calmly. "You've never pretended to be otherwise."

Teddy's face turned crimson. "I can't believe you said that."

"*Enough!*" Ollie thrust himself between the two and held up his hands. "Stop it, both of you. This is no time for us to argue among ourselves."

"You're right," Cyrus said, looking ashamed.

"But he said—"

"Teddy," Ollie said firmly, "we have more important things to focus on."

Teddy gave Ollie a quick belligerent look, then turned away scowling. "All right," she said grudgingly. "I didn't mean to start a fight."

"And I didn't mean to hurt your feelings," Cyrus said. "I'm sorry I called you self-centered."

Teddy shrugged. "I guess I am a *little* self-absorbed," she admitted.

"Now that *that's* settled," Beatrice said impatiently, "can we talk about what to do next? Because I don't mind telling you, I haven't a clue."

"The first thing we need to do is decide whether we're going through with this," Ollie said. "I suggest we take a vote."

"I vote yes," Teddy said promptly. "We continue on to Winter Wood."

She turned to look at Cyrus. There was a challenge in her eyes.

Cyrus hesitated, then said, "Yes. We go on."

Beatrice looked at Ollie's face, which was remarkably blank. "Yes," she said.

"That's a majority," Ollie said.

"We need a unanimous vote," Beatrice told him. "Vote the way you really feel."

Ollie took a deep breath. "I vote yes," he said.

"All right," Beatrice said. "Let's get on with it then."

The footprints led them up the gentle slope. Soon they reached the top of the hill.

"Well, there it is," Beatrice said.

They looked out across the fields. The hedge of thorns that surrounded Winter Wood stood no more than a quarter of a mile away. Even at this distance, it looked formidable, rising against the sky until it disappeared into the clouds. Awestruck, they stared at the hedge without speaking, then started down the hill toward it.

The hedge loomed over them as they approached, casting deep shadow over the surrounding countryside. There was something menacing about this living barricade with its daggerlike thorns. Beatrice could sense an evil presence that seemed to actually breathe and sigh as they came to stand before the hedge. There was no doubt that it was enchanted. And no doubt, either, that the tools they had brought would never be able to penetrate this fortress of malevolence.

Beatrice walked slowly up to the hedge. She wanted to inspect it at close range, to see if there was any weakness that might allow them to break through. But the dense growth formed a solid green wall, and the eight-inch thorns crisscrossed like barbed wire. Even a small child's hand could not have passed through the hedge without being slashed to the bone.

Beatrice pulled a hatchet from her backpack. The sharp blade gleamed. "This won't begin to cut through it," she said.

Ollie produced a second hatchet. "Well, we can try."

They swung their hatchets into the hedge. Instead of slicing through the wood, the blades bounced off like they were hitting rubber. Beatrice and Ollie moved to different locations. They tried swinging the hatchets overhand and underhand. Then Teddy and Cyrus took their turns. After nearly twenty minutes, they hadn't been able to cut away so much as a leaf. When Beatrice examined branches that she was certain had been struck by her blade, there wasn't a single cut or mark on the wood. In fact, any twig or trunk that the hatchet blade had touched seemed to have grown thicker.

"So much for chopping our way through," Ollie said, wiping his damp face on his sleeve.

"And we can't go over it, can we?" Cyrus said thoughtfully.

140

"According to *The Bailiwick Family History*, we would be lost in the clouds forever," Beatrice said.

They backed away from the hedge to sit down. Even Cayenne appeared subdued and sat quietly with Beatrice rather than stalking insects in the tall grass.

"All right," Ollie said. "We can't go over the hedge, and we can't go through. What about under?"

"What do you mean, *under*?" Teddy asked.

"We could dig a tunnel."

"We didn't bring shovels," Beatrice said. "Besides, you read in the family history that the hedge is twenty feet thick. It would take forever to dig a tunnel that long."

"And even if we could, it might cave in on us," Teddy added.

"Well, does anyone have a better idea?" Ollie asked, sounding faintly annoyed.

No one did. They sat staring at the hedge and thinking.

Beatrice shivered. "I believe cold air is seeping through," she said.

Ollie crawled closer to the hedge and held out his hand. "You're right. It's freezing. I guess that's just a taste of what we can expect if we ever do get inside Winter Wood."

They pulled out thick jackets, hats, and gloves from their backpacks and put them on. Even so, the air around them seemed to grow colder. Their teeth started to chatter and their noses turned pink.

Teddy was running her gloved hands up and down her arms to warm herself when she said suddenly, "Look at that! How cute."

She pointed at two mice running across the grass toward the hedge. They carried kernels of corn in their mouths.

"They must have a nest around here somewhere," Beatrice said.

Ollie, who had been lying in the grass, sat up. "Look where they're going," he said.

Everyone looked. The first mouse had already disappeared. The second was just approaching the hedge. Then he vanished—apparently, under it.

Ollie lay down flat on his belly to examine the base of the hedge.

"There's a very small tunnel through the hedge itself," he said. "Mouse size."

"Can you see all the way through?" Cyrus asked.

"No, just a couple of feet, then the tunnel curves."

As Ollie sat up, Cayenne made a dash for the hedge.

"Cayenne, *no!*" Beatrice exclaimed. "She's going after the mice. Cayenne, come back here!"

But the cat had already disappeared under the hedge.

Ollie lay down again and peered into the tunnel. "She's able to make it by sliding along on her belly," he said.

"Is she missing the thorns?" Beatrice asked anxiously.

"Just," Ollie said. "She isn't skinny, you know. Now she's turned the corner. I can't see her anymore."

"What do we do?" Beatrice came to look into the tunnel herself. "What if she gets trapped in there? What if Dally Rumpe does something terrible to her? Cayenne, come here! *Cayenne!*"

Beatrice called and cajoled and threatened. She stood

up and began to pace, imagining every awful thing that could happen to the cat, then she lay down again to look into the tunnel. "Cayenne, come out of there *now*!"

Beatrice sat up. She was flushed and close to tears.

Just then, they heard a faint "meow."

Beatrice dropped to her belly once more.

"I see her! She's creeping this way. Come on, Cayenne. Come on, sweetie."

When the cat finally reached the opening to the tunnel, Beatrice grabbed her and crawled away from the hedge. She held Cayenne close, murmuring endearments to her, and kissed the top of the cat's head. Several times.

Cyrus made a face. Ollie smiled. Teddy laughed aloud with relief.

"Too bad she can't talk," Ollie said, "and tell us if she made it to the other side."

"She *can* tell us," Beatrice said happily, and held up one of Cayenne's big paws. "There's ice in the fur between the paw pads. She walked on snow in Winter Wood."

Beatrice kissed Cayenne again. "Aren't you a brave, wonderful cat to risk your life just to show us?"

"Actually," Ollie said, "I think it was the mice that attracted her to the tunnel."

Teddy grinned at Ollie. "Always the stickler for accuracy, even if you do offend Beatrice and her cat."

"Too bad *we* aren't cats," Ollie mused. "Or mice."

"We could be," Cyrus said suddenly. "Or at least, the size of mice. I could shrink us."

"Of course!" Beatrice exclaimed.

"A perfect idea," Teddy said.

"But we can't all go, can we?" Ollie asked.

"Why not?" Teddy wanted to know.

"Ollie's right," Beatrice said. "At least one of us needs to stay here. That way, if the others don't make it, someone can tell our families what happened. There really isn't any reason for all four of us to go inside."

"I think two should go into Winter Wood," Cyrus said, "and two should remain here."

Ollie nodded. "That sounds sensible."

"And the two who stay here can keep Cayenne," Beatrice said. "I don't need to be worrying about her while I'm in there."

"So you've already decided," Teddy said sharply. "You'll be one of the two to go?"

"We don't have a choice," Beatrice replied. "I'm the one who has to say the spell."

"And I have to go," Cyrus added, "because Beatrice will need me to change her back to normal size after we're inside."

Teddy looked devastated.

"I know you had your heart set on going," Beatrice said to Teddy, "but I don't think it's fair to make Ollie stay alone. We don't even know how safe it is on *this* side of the hedge."

"Yeah, Teddy," Ollie said, looking a bit disappointed himself. "I'd feel better if you stayed with me."

"Like I could save you if Dally Rumpe appeared," Teddy mumbled, trying to smile.

"Then it's okay with you?" Beatrice asked.

Teddy nodded, and Ollie said, "Sure it's okay. And we'll keep Cayenne with us." He pulled the cat into his lap.

"So how long should they wait for us before going back to Skull House?" Cyrus asked.

"I don't know," Beatrice said. "Two days?"

None of them knew how much time Beatrice and Cyrus would need, but they agreed on two days.

"If we don't come back, tell Neva to notify the Witches' Executive Committee," Beatrice said.

"We won't have to do that," Ollie said firmly. "You'll be back."

"Of course we will," Beatrice replied. "We'll take flashlights and leave everything else here."

"But you should take the peaches," Teddy said.

"No, you and Ollie keep them. Cyrus and I probably won't have time to think about food."

Teddy flashed Cyrus a quick grin. "That'll be the day."

Beatrice searched for something else that needed to be said, but she couldn't think of anything. Now that it was time to leave Teddy and Ollie—not to mention Cayenne—she felt very unsure of herself.

"Don't take any unnecessary risks," Teddy said, sounding more worried now than disappointed.

"Not on your life," Cyrus responded, and looked at Beatrice. "Ready?"

Beatrice nodded quickly.

Cyrus placed his hand on her arm and began to chant:

> By the mysteries, one and all,
> Make us shrink from tall to small.
> Take us down to inches three,
> As my will, so mote it be!

Beatrice felt the strangest sensation, like she was being sucked down a drain, swirling around and around and around. When her head stopped spinning, she realized that she was standing among grass blades that were taller than she was. Beatrice was so small, she could have used an acorn as a soccer ball.

Beatrice looked up, and there were Teddy's and Ollie's faces appearing huge and terrible. Beatrice's foot would have fit easily into one of their nostrils.

Cyrus, on the other hand, was just her size.

"Shall we go now?" Beatrice asked him.

Waving good-bye to their friends, Beatrice and Cyrus stepped into the opening at the base of the hedge. It looked dark ahead, so Beatrice reached into her pocket and found that her flashlight had also been shrunk.

"This is so weird," she muttered.

"Nothing to it," Cyrus said. "I do it all the time."

13

Winter Wood

N ow that they were only three inches tall, Beatrice and Cyrus could easily walk side by side through the tunnel. Still, they were careful to avoid the hedge because the thorns appeared as long as saber blades, and just as deadly. They hadn't gone far when the two mice reappeared in the beams of their flashlights.

"They're huge," Beatrice said anxiously. "We wouldn't stand a chance if they attacked."

"Mice don't attack people," Cyrus scoffed.

"No—not *big* people!"

Just then, Beatrice felt a breeze stir behind her, and she heard something move through the tunnel. She turned, and in the sweeping arc of her flashlight saw a terrible creature. It had a huge head, fangs as long as her arm, and eyes that seemed on fire. Beatrice gasped.

Cyrus spun around and saw the monster behind Beatrice. He grabbed her arm and began to pull her away from the hideous thing.

But incredibly, Beatrice resisted! She was suddenly talking so fast, Cyrus couldn't make out a word she said.

And then it sounded to Cyrus as if she were *laughing*! He thought she must be in shock.

"Come *on*," he said, and jerked her arm more urgently.

Beatrice pulled away, and Cyrus watched in horror as the beast moved toward her. Then it lowered its monstrous head—and rubbed its face against her back. Gently.

Cyrus was flabbergasted. He didn't understand at all until he heard Beatrice say, "It's Cayenne, Cyrus. It's just my cat."

In their present miniature state, Cayenne looked as big as an elephant. And quite ghastly in the glare of their flashlights. But now Beatrice was scratching behind one giant ear and the terrifying monster was making sounds like a contented leaf blower.

"What are you doing here?" Beatrice asked the cat, and was rewarded with an affectionate butt from the huge head that almost knocked her down. "Easy, girl."

"How are you going to make her go back?" Cyrus asked.

But before Beatrice could answer, Cayenne spotted the mice. Her muscles tensed and she lowered her massive body into a position to pounce. No more than a foot away, the mice saw Cayenne and froze.

"Uh-oh," Cyrus muttered.

"Cayenne, go back to Ollie and Teddy," Beatrice said. "Right this minute. Do you hear me?"

Her eyes never moving from the mice, her tail twitching in anticipation, Cayenne ignored her mistress.

Beatrice was getting mad. She was under a lot of pressure, and she didn't feel like humoring a cat with an attitude. Just who was the witch around here, anyway?

"Cayenne, you are my familiar," Beatrice said sharply. "You will do as I say. Now, leave this instant."

Surprisingly, Cayenne's eyes left the mice and shifted to Beatrice.

"Go," Beatrice said. "*Now*."

Cayenne blinked. She rose slowly from her pounce position, looked at Beatrice's stern face, and turned around slowly in the tight space.

"That's a good familiar," Beatrice said briskly. "Go back to Ollie and Teddy."

Cayenne began to creep toward the tunnel entrance.

"Ollie, I'm sending Cayenne back!" Beatrice shouted as loudly as she could in her tiny voice.

Ollie heard her. "I'm sorry, Beatrice!" Even at a distance, his voice echoed like thunder. "I won't let her get away again."

Beatrice watched until Cayenne reached the end of the tunnel. She saw hands reach out and pick up the cat.

"I've got her," Ollie called. "I'll tie my belt to her collar, so she won't be able to get away."

"Thanks, Ollie!" Beatrice shouted. Then she flashed her light in the direction of the mice. They were watching her intently.

"You're safe," she told them. "But be careful if you go outside the hedge. The cat's still there."

Cyrus was also watching her. "Do you think they can understand?"

"I don't know," Beatrice said. "But not much would surprise me at this point."

The mice looked at Beatrice a moment longer, then glanced at each other, twitched their whiskers, and ran back into the tunnel.

Beatrice let out a long breath. Then she grinned at Cyrus. "Ready to move on?" she asked.

"As ready as I'll ever be."

They walked for a long time. There were only silence and darkness and the glow of their flashlights around them. When they finally reached the end of the tunnel, it came as a surprise because there was no circle of light to announce that they had arrived at the other side of the hedge. They looked out of the passageway into blackness.

"The book called Winter Wood 'the land of midnight,'" Beatrice whispered.

"Appropriate, I'd say," Cyrus whispered back.

Beatrice stepped out of the tunnel, and immediately sank over her head into something wet and cold. It was snow. Then Cyrus descended into the drift with her.

"I think it's time to change us back to normal size," he said, and began to chant:

> *By the mysteries, one and all,*
> *Make us grow from small to tall.*
> *Let us from this spell be free,*
> *As my will, so mote it be.*

Beatrice felt the same dizzying swirl that she had experienced when Cyrus shrank her. Only this time she spun around and then popped up like a jack-in-the-box.

Beatrice sat down and rested her head on her knees until the dizziness receded. When she looked up, she realized that she was full-size again, and that she was sitting in several inches of snow, as was Cyrus. Her bottom was numb.

"We'd better move if we don't want to freeze," Beatrice said.

She stood up and looked around. There was a full moon, and the purple-black sky was filled with stars.

"I don't think we need the flashlights," Beatrice said. "We'll be less conspicuous without them."

They turned off the lights and allowed their eyes to adjust to the darkness. Soon Beatrice could see quite well. It was a desolate place, and yet, starkly beautiful. The moon spread a cold metallic light across snow-covered fields. Leafless trees rose like bent skeletons from the frozen earth. There was nothing to disturb the silence except for the rustling of dead grasses in the wind and the howling of wolves in the distance.

They began to walk. The snow crunched under their shoes. The cold soon made their nostrils stick together, and they were forced to breathe by gulping air through their mouths. There was no sign that people lived here, but the wolves continued to serenade them, and they heard the occasional cry of a wildcat.

Suddenly something large and white swooped down, barely missing Beatrice's and Cyrus's heads before it flew away to perch in a nearby tree. It was a snow owl. Beatrice stopped to stare as the elegant creature turned its head to peer back at her.

They trudged on through the snow and the darkness. Beatrice lost track of time. She just knew that she was tired. And very cold. Her legs were wobbly, and she couldn't feel her feet at all. She wasn't sure how much longer she could go on, but what choice did they have? If they sat down to rest, they might freeze to death, and no one would ever know.

Cyrus stumbled, and Beatrice reached out to catch him.

"I'd give anything to see Skull House right now," he mumbled. "To have a mug of Personal Taste Brew and be in my warm troll bed again."

"I know."

"I'm so tired," Cyrus said.

"Me, too. But we can't—"

Suddenly Beatrice stopped.

"What is it?" Cyrus asked weakly.

"I see a light!"

"Where?"

"Over there. See? It's a window!"

Beatrice forgot that she was exhausted. She started walking toward the light. Cyrus plodded along behind her.

"You're right," he said, panting as he struggled to keep up. "It's a cottage. I can see the slope of the roof."

"And there's smoke rising from the chimney!" Beatrice exclaimed. Then she came to a halt. "Wait a minute," she said softly. "What if this is a trick? What if Dally Rumpe's inside watching for us?"

"We'll be quiet," Cyrus said. "He won't hear us."

"He may already know we're here."

But Beatrice realized that they couldn't continue to wander around in the dark and the cold. They had to find a place to get warm, and someone to ask about Rhona.

They stopped behind a screen of pine trees not far from the cottage. Even by moonlight, Beatrice could see that the dwelling was no more than a shack, with light showing between uneven boards and through a thin piece of cloth over the window. But there was a fire burning in the hearth, and Beatrice smelled something cooking. It made her mouth water.

"You think Dally Rumpe might feed us before he kills us?" Cyrus asked.

"Funny," Beatrice muttered. "You stay here. I'm going to sneak up to the window and see if I can look inside."

"The window's too high."

"I can climb up on that pile of wood."

Beatrice started toward the cottage. She heard Cyrus behind her and turned around. "I told you to wait," she said.

"I didn't feel like it," Cyrus said. "We're in this together, remember?"

"Oh, all right. Just try to be more quiet."

They reached the woodpile. Beatrice looked at the window above their heads. "There's a tear in the cloth," she said. "If I can get up there, I'll be able to see inside."

"I'll give you a boost."

Cyrus laced his fingers together and hoisted Beatrice up. She stepped carefully onto the woodpile, but not carefully enough. A piece of wood rolled out from under her foot and went clattering to the ground. Startled by the noise, Cyrus jumped, and both he and Beatrice lost their balance. They landed in a heap on the frozen ground.

The door to the cottage swung open. A very large man

stepped outside. He spotted Beatrice and Cyrus as they scrambled to their feet, and he reached for a piece of wood.

"What is it?" came a woman's frightened voice from inside.

"Intruders," was the man's short reply. "No need to worry. I'll take care of them."

He raised the length of wood over his head and started toward Beatrice and Cyrus.

"No!" Beatrice cried out. "We aren't here to hurt you. We want to help."

The door creaked as it opened wider. The woman and several children peeked out from behind it.

"Are you here to spy for Dally Rumpe?" the man asked harshly.

Beatrice could see his face in the dim light from the door. He was watchful and angry. But she realized that he also looked frightened.

"We've come to break Dally Rumpe's spell," Beatrice said. "We want to free Rhona—and everyone else who lives in Winter Wood."

The man eyed her with suspicion. "Why would you risk your life to do that? Or are you so powerful that it isn't a risk at all?"

"We have very little power," Beatrice admitted. "But it's written in my family history that I must try to break the spell. My name is Beatrice Bailiwick. Have you heard of Bromwich of Bailiwick?"

"Everyone's heard of Bromwich. But how do I know you're telling the truth?"

"You'll just have to trust her," Cyrus said. "We really are here to help you."

The man lowered his arm slowly but held onto his weapon. "It's true that it's written in the book," he said. "Others have tried—and failed."

"I know that," Beatrice said. "But if you could take us to Rhona—"

The woman moved out from behind the door. "Oh, no," she said fearfully. "He can't do that."

"Dally Rumpe might be out there," the man said, gazing off into the darkness. He glanced back at Beatrice, looking ashamed. "He can take any shape he pleases, so you never know. In fact," he said, his voice growing suspicious, "you might be Dally Rumpe yourself, here to test us."

Neither Beatrice nor Cyrus said anything. They just looked at the man and waited.

"He'll kill us if we help you," the woman said, and began to cry.

"Aren't you tired of living in fear?" Beatrice asked her. "In cold and darkness?"

"Yes," the woman said faintly, "but we can't help you."

The man stared hard at Beatrice for a moment. Finally he said in a low voice, "Continue on past all the cottages. You'll see a small stone house just beyond. That's where Rhona lives. And there's a fierce, fire-breathing dragon called Spitfire who guards her. Sometimes he leaves, but even then, he seems to know when anyone comes near the house. I'm afraid you've come this far just to die in flames."

"But that won't be all," the woman said sharply. "You'll annoy Spitfire no end, and once you're dead, we'll be left to deal with his ill humor. He'll shoot fire at our thatch roofs and stomp through our meager stores of grain." The woman glared at Beatrice. "His stomping might even cause an avalanche in the hills."

"It's true," the man said sadly. "You're doing us no favor, Witch of Bailiwick."

Before Beatrice could respond, the man and woman went back inside and the door slammed shut.

14

Spitfire the Dragon

They walked past a dozen or more silent cottages. Beatrice looked at the lighted windows, expecting to see some sign of life—perhaps the face of a child peeking out—but none appeared. It seemed that these people were too frightened to even look out their windows at the winter moon. *What a terrible way to live*, Beatrice thought, and felt a fierce anger toward the sorcerer who had created this hellish place.

They moved slowly now, their legs aching with exhaustion, their bodies numb with cold. Beatrice worried that they were in no condition to confront a dragon, or whatever else Winter Wood might present. They were in desperate need of food and a warm fire.

But there was the house, just ahead. Beatrice could see it clearly because a lantern burned outside the door, the flame casting fitful shadows across the stone walls. Rhona waited on the other side of those walls. *We're too close to turn back now*, Beatrice thought.

Beatrice and Cyrus crouched behind some low bushes,

where they could watch the house without being seen. Fifteen minutes passed, and there was no sign of a dragon. Like the rest of the village, the house was silent. But smoke curled from the chimney, and the two front windows showed threads of light around the shutters.

Shifting her weight from one frozen leg to the other, Beatrice whispered, "It would be too easy to just walk up to the front door and go in. I'm sure we'd be stopped."

"Or eaten," Cyrus replied.

"Let's go around to the back of the house and see if there's another way in." Beatrice paused, thinking. "Maybe you should shrink us again. We wouldn't be as noticeable. But wait," she added hastily. "Let's stand on this flat stone so we won't sink into the snow."

Cyrus cast his spell, and they shrank to three inches tall. After her head stopped spinning, Beatrice gazed across the yard to the house.

"It looks as though someone has dug a path in the snow around the side of the house," she said. "Let's follow it. But be ready to jump into a snowdrift if we see or hear anything."

They darted across some dry flagstones to the dirt path. The ground was damp and their feet were soon covered with mud, but that was better than falling into snow over their heads.

Beatrice led the way around the corner of the house. That's when they saw it, no more than twenty feet away. The dragon! And it was absolutely *nothing* like Neva's puppylike stray.

The dragon was so tall, its head brushed the eaves of the house. Its green and silver scales gleamed in the dim light. Beautiful, was Beatrice's first thought. Terrifying, her second. The dragon was obviously on guard, tossing its enormous head this way and that while its silver eyes scanned the landscape like searchlights, missing nothing.

"Go back around the corner of the house," Beatrice whispered. "Slowly."

But the dragon had already seen them. It drew itself up to its full incredible height and roared. With the roar came a stream of fire that instantly melted a six-foot strip of snow. Which explained the bare path around the house.

But Beatrice didn't stop to consider the dragon's usefulness for snow removal. She started to run toward the front of the house. Cyrus followed at a gallop.

The beast came after them. Its stomping shook the earth. A tremor that felt to Beatrice like an earthquake sent her tumbling to the ground. Cyrus reached out to pull her to her feet, but it was too late. The horrible thing was nearly upon them. It was throwing back its head, preparing to spit more fire. And this time Beatrice and Cyrus would be directly in the path of the inferno.

There was no time to plan. Beatrice began to mutter:

> *Circle of magic, hear my plea.*
> *Blowing winds,*
> *Blinding snow,*
> *These, I ask you, bring to me.*

Snow began to fall. A fierce wind howled through the trees. By the time Beatrice had staggered to her feet, a blizzard was swirling around them. The dragon was so huge—not to mention, iridescent—Beatrice could still see its great gleaming bulk through the snow. It was batting angrily at the frozen crystals that blew into its eyes.

With the creature thus occupied, Beatrice and Cyrus made it to the front of the house. But the beast was still after them. The earth trembled again, even more so now because the dragon was furious. Beatrice felt a sudden warmth at her back. She turned and saw a spray of fire coming around the corner. The blizzard had only given them a brief reprieve.

Beatrice was pulling Cyrus along the base of the house —her mind spinning as she tried to think of something that would save them—when she discovered a small hole in the foundation. With the dragon on their heels, and the blinding snow swirling around them, Beatrice slipped through the crevice and jerked Cyrus in after her.

Beatrice and Cyrus stumbled deeper into the hole, but they had only gone a short way when they ran into solid stone. It was too dark to see anything. Beatrice considered turning on her flashlight, but she was afraid the dragon would be able to see the light. Then she heard another roar, and saw the flames outside the hole. Snow around the foundation melted instantly, and water began to pour in. Beatrice felt it covering her feet, then rising to her ankles.

"Beatrice, it's no use!" Cyrus exclaimed. "We're going to drown."

"There has to be some way out," Beatrice responded, and began to feel along the wall for an opening.

She might never have found it on her own. But as she moved through the darkness, Beatrice saw a light out of the corner of her eye. She turned instinctively toward the brightness and found herself staring into a small tunnel that was on higher ground and still dry. Someone with a tiny lantern was moving down the passageway toward them.

It was a creature no larger than Beatrice and Cyrus were now—a man with a red wool stocking cap and scraggly chin whiskers—and he was riding on a mouse! Behind him was another tiny bearded man astride a mouse.

"This way, this way," one of the little men said in an agitated voice. "We'll help you."

With the water now waist high, Beatrice and Cyrus had no choice but to trust the strange pair. The men had jumped off the backs of the mice and were holding out their hands. Beatrice and Cyrus started toward them.

Walking through the deep water wasn't easy, but finally, Beatrice felt the surprisingly strong grip of a gnarled little hand around hers. The men fairly yanked Beatrice and Cyrus into the tunnel. Beatrice's exhausted legs folded and she collapsed at the feet of her small rescuer, who peered down at her with kindly concern.

"I'm Snuffers and this is Paddy," the little man said.

"Are you—elves?" Beatrice guessed.

"Gnomes," the man answered. "But there's no time to exchange family histories. We have to move on before the water reaches us."

"Right," Paddy said. "Climb on and we'll take you to higher ground."

"You mean—get up on this mouse?" Beatrice didn't know about that.

"Do you see anything else to ride?" Snuffers demanded.

"The mice are grateful," Paddy said. "They want to pay their debt to you."

"What debt?" Cyrus asked.

"You saved them from the cat-beast."

"These are the mice we followed into Winter Wood," Beatrice said to Cyrus.

"Just *hop on*!" Snuffers ordered.

Beatrice crawled onto the back of one mouse and Cyrus seated himself on the other one. A gnome climbed up behind each of them and picked up reins no thicker than sewing thread. The mice spun around and took off! As swiftly as racehorses, the rodents ascended the steep passageway, and soon emerged into a large open space with a dirt floor.

"We're in the root cellar under Good Witch Rhona's house," Snuffers said.

"You know Rhona?" Beatrice asked quickly.

"*Everyone* in Winter Wood knows Rhona."

"But we know her better than most," Paddy said. "We come in the way we just brought you and visit from time to time."

Beatrice couldn't believe her good fortune. "Then we can reach Rhona from here?"

"Certainly," Paddy said.

"But why do you want to see Rhona?" Snuffers asked, a hint of suspicion in his voice.

"We've come to set her free," Cyrus said.

The gnomes looked from Cyrus to Beatrice.

"Is this true?" Snuffers asked.

Beatrice nodded. "We're here to break Dally Rumpe's spell."

Paddy didn't appear convinced. "It's been fifty years or more since anyone's tried."

Cyrus gave him a searching look. "I've been wondering about the others," he said. "What happened to them exactly?"

"You don't want to know," Paddy replied, so emphatically that Cyrus decided not to pursue the matter.

"I think we can trust them," Snuffers said to Paddy. "If they were working for Dally Rumpe, they'd be able to take better care of themselves."

Paddy considered this, then nodded. "You're probably right. Dally Rumpe wouldn't tolerate subordinates who couldn't even save themselves from drowning."

Beatrice was mildly insulted, and meant to tell them so, but then Paddy said, "All right. We'll take you to Rhona."

"You will?" Beatrice's indignation began to fade.

"And we'll help you all we can," Snuffers added, his tone suggesting that Beatrice and Cyrus were in dire need of *someone's* help.

Beatrice was so happy at the prospect of being face-to-face with Rhona, she chose to ignore his implication and turned instead to the mice, who were watching her intently with their bright little eyes.

"Thank you for saving our lives," she said to them. "We'll never forget you."

The mice looked at each other and then back at Beatrice, and their whiskers began to twitch.

"They said it was their pleasure," Snuffers said. "Now, come along."

Beatrice and Cyrus followed the gnomes up a gnome-size staircase. They climbed and climbed, until they finally reached an immense door with a two-inch crack beneath it.

"Duck your heads," Snuffers said, and crawled under the door. The others followed.

The gnomes led Beatrice and Cyrus down a long corridor and through an arched doorway. They found themselves in a cozy room with a fire burning in the hearth. A young woman with long black hair was sitting beside the window. She had opened the shutter and was watching Beatrice's blizzard while she cracked walnuts.

"Good Witch Rhona," Snuffers said, "pardon me, but Paddy and I have brought visitors."

The woman turned toward them. She wasn't beautiful—as Dr. Meadowmouse had been forced to admit—but her face showed intelligence and kindness. *And despair*, Beatrice thought. Then Rhona saw the gnomes, and Beatrice and Cyrus, and the sadness left her eyes. When she smiled, she *was* very nearly beautiful.

"Snuffers, Paddy, how good to see you," Rhona said. "I was just cracking nuts for a cake. You must stay and help me eat it. You and your friends." Her dark eyes swept over Beatrice and Cyrus's jeans and hiking shoes. "You don't look like any gnomes I've ever seen," she added.

"We aren't gnomes, we're witches," Beatrice said. "Cyrus, make us normal size again."

And he did. Rhona and the gnomes were astonished to see their small acquaintances suddenly grow and grow until they were nearly as tall as Rhona herself.

Bromwich's daughter had turned pale. "You're here to break the spell," she said softly. Her hopeful eyes met Beatrice's. "You're a Bailiwick witch, aren't you?"

Beatrice nodded. "I'm Beatrice Bailiwick. And this is

my friend Cyrus. But there isn't much time. I have to repeat the counterspell in your presence."

Rhona, Snuffers, Paddy, and even Cyrus watched in awe as Beatrice began to recite the words that she had so painstakingly memorized:

> *By the power of the north,*
> *By the beauty of the night,*
> *Release this circle, I do implore,*
> *Make all that's wrong revert to right.*

Suddenly the house began to shake. It was the dragon roaring outside the door. Beatrice closed her mind to the terrible sounds, and to the floor trembling beneath her feet. She had to stay focused on the spell. She had to keep reciting the words.

> *By the power of the north,*
> *By the spirit of the wood—*

There was pounding on the door, but Beatrice scarcely heard it. The door splintered. Rhona dropped the bowl of nuts she was holding, and the gnomes scurried to hide under the edge of the carpet. The dragon crashed into the house. And Beatrice chanted:

> *Release this circle, I do implore,*
> *Make all that's evil revert to good.*

The dragon peered at them from the front hall. The top of its head touched the ceiling. Its enormous tail whipped angrily, breaking the staircase railing to bits.

By the power of the north,
By the chant of witch's song,
Release this circle, I do implore,
Make all that's weak revert to strong.

The horrible creature lowered its head and lumbered into the room. Chairs and tables were crushed and left in splinters. Rhona and Cyrus stared at the beast in horror, but Beatrice had her eyes squeezed tightly shut, and kept saying the words over the sounds of destruction around her.

The dragon roared, so close that Beatrice's eyes opened involuntarily and she faltered in her recitation. The creature breathed out flames and the draperies caught fire. Rhona began to beat at the blaze with the skirt of her robes, while Cyrus used his jacket to smother the flames.

Beatrice had backed into a corner. She was saying the words to the counterspell as rapidly as she could, while she watched the monster take a giant step toward her. There wasn't time to finish the spell, Beatrice feared. In one breath the dragon could silence her forever. But she couldn't give up. Maybe there would be a miracle. It would take that now to save them.

The dragon took another step, and Beatrice—still reciting the spell—noticed that the beast looked different. Something in its face was changing. The silver eyes were turning darker, the long muzzle was disappearing. Then Beatrice saw that the dragon's body was shrinking and taking on a new shape. The fire-breathing dragon, she realized in alarm, was becoming human.

Yes, it was a man's face that was beginning to materialize. A nose, two eyes, a mouth—Beatrice gasped. *No, it couldn't be*, she thought, as the corners of the mouth lifted into a smile—a terrible menacing smile that sent icy shivers down Beatrice's back.

That was when it occurred to Beatrice that she had forgotten the rest of the words to the counterspell. She struggled to remember, but her mind was blank of everything but shock and fear.

The transformed dragon laughed cruelly and said, "You look quite stunned, my dear. But then I don't imagine that you expected to see me here."

15

Dally Rumpe Unmasked

"You," Beatrice said weakly.

She was staring into the narrowed eyes of Roger Middlemarch.

Cyrus came to stand beside Beatrice, his face streaked with soot from putting out the fire. "Then you weren't really looking for the Higgledy-piggledy Moondust Brownie at all," he said.

The man laughed again. "Of course not, but wasn't it a good cover?" he said, obviously delighted with himself. "No one would suspect boring old Roger of being—" He paused, his eyes glittering and his lips twitching, before he finally said, "*Dally Rumpe*, the greatest sorcerer who ever lived!"

Beatrice cringed, but she wouldn't allow herself to fall apart. She had to think! To remember the words to the spell.

"What about Matilda?" Beatrice asked, stalling for time. "Does she know who you really are?"

Dally Rumpe sniggered. "Are you kidding? Poor Matilda doesn't know what day it is most of the time. I met her at Witch U after taking on my Roger Middlemarch identity, and she proved useful." He grinned wickedly. "She's been such a devoted little gofer!"

The man's arrogance made Beatrice sick, but she couldn't dwell on that. The words! What were the *words*?

"I must say," the sorcerer remarked, "you've been more of a challenge than I expected. Mark it up to beginner's luck, I suppose. Of course, I could have done away with all of you at any time."

"Why didn't you then," Cyrus demanded, "if you're so powerful?"

Dally Rumpe glared at Cyrus and said coldly, "Because I enjoyed playing with you. I've gotten some good laughs watching you all struggle and think you're winning—when I knew it was just a matter of time before I'd have you trembling and begging for your lives."

"I don't hear anyone begging," Cyrus said stoutly.

Beatrice was grateful to Cyrus. For being brave and for keeping Dally Rumpe occupied. The words of the spell were on the tip of her tongue. If she could think for just a minute—

"You have a big mouth, don't you?" the sorcerer said to Cyrus.

Rhona took a step toward Dally Rumpe. "Let them go," she said wearily. "They didn't win. My father and my sisters and I are still your prisoners. Bailiwick is still under your control. You can afford to be generous."

"Me, be generous?" Dally Rumpe howled with laughter. "And ruin an evil reputation that's taken centuries to build?"

Beatrice saw the gnomes slide out from under the carpet. They moved silently behind Dally Rumpe toward the bowl Rhona had dropped.

"You read the letter from Dr. Thigpin," Beatrice said, trying to divert the sorcerer's attention from Snuffers and Paddy.

"It wasn't very bright of you to mention the letter in the lobby that night with everyone standing around," Dally Rumpe said. "*Anyone* could have heard you. As I did. So while you were guzzling Personal Taste Brew, I went to your room and read the letter. Thaddeus Thigpin's more stupid than I imagined," the sorcerer said with a sneer, "thinking that you and your bungling little friends actually stood a chance against me. *Amazing!*"

While he boasted and swaggered, Beatrice watched out of the corner of her eye as the gnomes edged toward him.

"And you were the one who left the message for me in the library," she said quickly, "the warning written in blood."

Dally Rumpe bared his teeth in a hideous smile. "Actually, it was written with Matilda's lipstick. All I had available on such short notice. But the enchanted book was a nice touch, I thought."

"Except that it didn't work," Cyrus remarked, with a grin almost as nasty as the sorcerer's. "Your warning didn't scare anyone away, did it?"

Dally Rumpe's face darkened and his eyes glittered with anger. "You're a very foolish witch, did you know that? And I've become quite bored with your chatter. It's time to show you how powerful I really am."

He took a step toward Beatrice and Cyrus. That's when the gnomes tilted the bowl of nuts and sent them spilling across the floor. Some rolled under Dally Rumpe's feet, causing him to lose his footing. Arms flailing as he tried to regain his balance, the sorcerer slipped and slid— and then crashed to the floor.

Beatrice grabbed hold of Rhona's hand and sprinted for the door. Cyrus dashed after them.

"Save yourselves," Rhona was pleading as Beatrice pulled her across the debris that had once been a staircase. "He's too powerful—we can't defeat him!"

Oh, no? Beatrice thought as she tugged Rhona over the threshold and outside into the freezing night. Dally Rumpe's evil had made her angry—no, *furious!*—and she was determined not to give up without a fight.

They were running through the snow as quickly as they could. Fearing that Dally Rumpe was in close pursuit, Beatrice longed to look behind her. But she didn't dare slow down and give him even a second's advantage.

Breathless, his teeth chattering convulsively, Cyrus stammered into Beatrice's ear, "Wh-where are we g-going?"

Beatrice just shook her head. She didn't *know* where they were going. There was no safe place in Winter Wood.

For an instant, Beatrice felt her resolve begin to crumble. She looked back over her shoulder, fully expecting to find Dally Rumpe breathing down her neck. She did see him—or at least, she saw the dark bulk of a man that she assumed was him—but he was still some distance back. Beatrice paused long enough to observe that he was moving with unaccountable slowness, and that he even seemed to be hopping around a bit, first on one foot and then on the other. His behavior was mystifying until she noticed the two small creatures darting at his feet—apparently attacking him—and then scurrying away before he could step on them. That's when she understood. *The mice!* Beatrice was so touched by this unexpected act of loyalty and bravery that her own courage was rekindled. *No,* she thought, *we can't give up yet.*

Rhona was gasping for breath. She clutched at Beatrice's arm and said again, "Save yourselves. I can't go any farther."

"Yes, you can," Beatrice said sharply. But she was out of breath and beginning to slow down herself.

They had passed all the cottages except the last one, where the man had told them how to find Rhona. Not knowing what else to do, Beatrice ran to the door of the darkened house and began to pound on it.

"Go away!" came the command from inside.

"I won't go away," Beatrice responded. "I have Rhona with me. If you can't find the courage to help yourselves, won't you at least try to save her?"

Beatrice heard low voices behind the door—the man and his wife disagreeing. She looked back and saw that Dally Rumpe had gained ground. He was halfway down the row of cottages now and coming swiftly toward them.

Beatrice pounded on the door again until pain shot through her clenched fist. And the door opened.

The man held up a lit torch and peered past her at Rhona's face. "Get inside!" he said gruffly.

As Beatrice pushed Rhona through the doorway, she heard from behind her an angry bellow. Then

Dally Rumpe's incensed voice was screaming, *"Witch of Bailiwick—it's all over for you!"*

It would have been over—Beatrice certainly thought that it was—but at that instant, the quivering flame of the cottager's torch caught her eye. Without even realizing what she was doing, Beatrice grabbed the torch and flung it out the doorway in the direction of Dally Rumpe.

The sorcerer leaped aside and the torch fell into the snow, hissing and steaming as its flame was doused out. But Dally Rumpe had been caught off guard. He slipped on the icy ground and fell flat.

As she stared down at the man sprawled in the snow, Beatrice felt her exhaustion and terror dissolve. And as if by magic, the words to the spell came back to her. Joyfully, she began to chant:

> *By the power of the north,*
> *By the goodness of the dove,*
> *Release the circle, I do implore,*
> *Make all that's hateful revert to love.*

The sorcerer's eyes rolled back into his head. His face was contorted with rage. He tried to stand, but it was too late. Beatrice sang out:

> *Heed this charm, attend to me,*
> *As my word, so mote it be!*

As soon as the last word was spoken, the black night sky seemed to split apart, allowing brilliant sunlight to burst through. A warm breeze brought with it the sounds of birds singing. New leaves began to unfurl on bare trees and blades of grass poked through the rapidly melting snow.

Dally Rumpe was writhing in pain. His eyes found Beatrice's and held them.

"What a poor excuse for a witch you are," the sorcerer hissed. "It was all luck. But it's not over yet."

His image began to fade, until all that remained of the great Dally Rumpe was a swirl of mist. As the mist rose into the air and floated away, Beatrice heard his words again.

"It's not over yet."

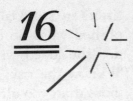

16

Halloween Eve

hona lifted her face to the sun and smiled at its warmth. "This is the Bailiwick I remember," she said softly.

Beatrice gazed at her transformed surroundings in wonder. The grass seemed too brilliantly green to be real. The light was golden, as if sunbeams had been ground to a fine dust and then flung into the air. She could hear the sounds of a lone flute and of sweet high voices singing words in a language she didn't understand. How remarkable, she mused, and how *right* that Bailiwick would turn out to be the magical place in her dreams.

Rhona sighed, and then turned to Beatrice and Cyrus. "How can I ever thank you?" she asked.

"No need for thanks," Cyrus muttered, and stared at his feet.

"You realize that it's only Winter Wood that's been released from Dally Rumpe's spell," Beatrice said to Rhona. "He can never set foot on this land again, but the other parts of the kingdom remain enchanted."

Rhona's expression was somber. "Yes, my father and

sisters are still Dally Rumpe's prisoners. But you've accomplished what no other Bailiwick witch has been able to do," she added, with a sudden glimmer of hope in her eyes. "I know the risks are great, and I can't expect you to do more than you already have . . ." Her voice trailed off and she looked away, apparently embarrassed by having to ask for Beatrice's help.

Beatrice was equally uncomfortable. She had no idea what the Witches' Executive Committee would direct them to do next, so how could she make any promises? Then it occurred to her that the committee's plans really didn't matter. Even if Thaddeus Thigpin ordered her to end the Quest that very day, she couldn't. Not after meeting Rhona and seeing the terrible suffering that Dally Rumpe had inflicted.

Beatrice sighed. "I can't say when or how," she said to Rhona, "but my friends and I will try to help your father and sisters. You have my word."

She was rewarded with a radiant smile from Rhona and a grin from Cyrus.

Then Beatrice's attention was drawn to the villagers, who were beginning to come out of their cottages. They looked dazed at first, then astounded as they saw that spring had returned to Winter Wood—and started to realize what this meant. They moved toward Rhona, who had been regarded as their captive princess all these years, and a symbol of all that was good. The villagers had never seen Bromwich's daughter before, but they knew her instinctively, and came to stand before her with joyful hearts.

Rhona announced that Dally Rumpe's spell on Winter Wood had finally been broken. "Two good and powerful witches are in our midst," she said, beaming at Beatrice and Cyrus. "We owe our freedom to them."

The villagers applauded and cheered. They started to chant, "*Speech, speech, speech!*"

Beatrice's face turned crimson at this unexpected display of gratitude and affection. Wholly undeserved, she felt. It had been the cottager who had shown them the way, and the gnomes and the mice who had saved them from drowning and taken them to Rhona. All Beatrice had done was repeat a few words from *The Bailiwick Family History*—and she had very nearly messed that up!

Beatrice glanced expectantly at Cyrus, who could usually be counted on to speak up happily if given half a chance. But Cyrus appeared as overwhelmed as she by the attention, leaving Beatrice little choice but to speak to the villagers herself. She stammered out that she and Cyrus had done very little, that it had been the villagers' own neighbor who had defied Dally Rumpe by helping them, and Paddy and Snuffers and two Winter Wood mice who had shown tremendous courage and made it possible for the spell to be broken. Her words only served to convince the villagers further that here was a witch who possessed true greatness, not to mention a most endearing humility. They cheered all the more and moved in closer to shyly touch Beatrice's hand and pat Cyrus on the back. Amid so much spontaneous goodwill, Beatrice and Cyrus could only wait it out, blushing and shaking hands until the crowd quieted down.

Finally, the man who had helped them stepped forward and said with grave dignity, "My name is Torquil. It would be my honor to serve you in any way I can." Then he shouted to the other villagers, "We must prepare them a feast to show our gratitude!"

The villagers all began to speak at once in wholehearted agreement.

Cyrus looked pleased at the idea of food, but Beatrice had other plans. "We thank you for your generosity," she told the crowd, "but we're anxious to see our friends and families. They'll be worried until they know we're safe. Could you help us find our way back?"

"We'll *take* you," Rhona said promptly, and the others nodded and said, "Yes, of course, certainly we'll take you."

"I will personally escort you," Torquil said.

"I wish you could stay," Rhona told them, "but I understand that you need to go home to your families. Just remember that you'll always have friends in Bailiwick. I'm here if you ever need me."

Torquil hitched horses to a wagon, and Beatrice and Cyrus climbed in. The villagers gathered around them, calling out their good wishes. As the wagon pulled away, Beatrice noticed two tiny men among the villagers' feet, vigorously waving their arms and grinning. It was Paddy and Snuffers, sitting on the backs of the mice.

Beatrice leaned out of the wagon and waved in return. *"Thank you! Good-bye! I hope we'll see you again someday!"*

She kept waving until the village was no more than a speck in the distance.

The wagon lurched and rattled across a lush green landscape that bore no resemblance to the one they had traveled through to find Rhona. That journey had been a long and difficult one, but the return trip seemed to take no time at all. They had just crested a grassy knoll when Beatrice caught sight of Teddy at the bottom of the hill. Beside her stood Ollie, with Cayenne perched on his shoulder.

The hedge was gone. Beatrice looked for any remaining signs of the wall of thorns and found nothing but tender shoots of new spring grass.

They arrived back at Skull House on the evening before Halloween. Neva met them at the door and hugged each in turn.

"I'm *proud* of you!" she exclaimed.

Beatrice was startled. "You know what happened in Winter Wood?" she asked.

"Of course." Neva beamed. "Witches' grapevine. Oh, and the Witches' Executive Committee is here to congratulate you, too."

Beatrice hadn't expected this. She didn't know whether to be pleased or nervous. What if they classified her as a Classical witch? What if they didn't? It was all so confusing. Beatrice wasn't sure *what* she wanted.

Teddy looked troubled, as well. "They won't change my classification," she said mournfully. "I didn't do anything. You and Cyrus were the ones who took the risks and broke the spell."

"It was a team effort," Beatrice said.

"I don't think the Executive Committee will see it that way," Teddy replied.

"Classifications don't matter," Ollie said. He had been smiling ever since he spotted Beatrice's red head in the back of the villager's wagon. "I'm just glad we're all together again."

"And I'm glad that we're back at Skull House where there's plenty to eat," Cyrus said. "I'm starving."

"Come with me," Neva said promptly. "All of you."

She led them through the house and out the door to the backyard, where a party was in full swing. Tables had been set up across the lawn under the soft glow of fairy-lights. Birdella and Amarantha came running and made a fuss over the travelers.

"Find them a table," Neva said. "And fill their plates with a little of everything."

In no time, Beatrice and her friends were stuffing themselves with devil dogs, hexburgers, brimstone baked beans, fury fries, and phantom punch. For dessert, they had devil's food cake.

Cyrus was starting on his third piece of cake when the Witches' Executive Committee came en masse to the table.

"Please, don't get up," Thaddeus Thigpin said. "We just want to welcome you back."

"And?" Aura Featherstone prompted him.

Dr. Thigpin frowned. "And congratulate you on a job well done."

"Well *done!*" Leopold Meadowmouse exclaimed happily.

"Well done, indeed." Most Worthy Piddle, wearing black robes and a black hat adorned with golden serpents, had stopped at their table. "But I hope you know when to leave well enough alone," he added sternly to Beatrice.

"Still, it's all rather astounding. Perhaps you'll be allowed to study with me one day."

Luckily, the witch tutor moved on before Beatrice had to think of a polite response.

Then Peregrine stepped out from behind Dr. Featherstone and looked timidly at Beatrice. He was actually smiling.

"I knew you could do it," he said. "Never doubted it for a minute."

Beatrice smiled back at Peregrine. Her witch adviser was definitely growing on her.

"All of you are to be commended," Dr. Featherstone said. "You showed tremendous courage and resourcefulness, not to mention strength of character. We're all quite proud of you. And there's something else that Dr. Thigpin wanted to say." She looked at the Institute director. "Isn't there, Thaddeus?"

It was obvious to Beatrice that their success at Winter Wood hadn't impressed Dr. Thigpin one bit. He still seemed to think this was a waste of his time.

"You did well," Dr. Thigpin muttered, then added with emphasis, "but this is only the *beginning* of the test. Once you're further along, we'll consider your classification, Beatrice Bailiwick. As well as those of your friends."

Beatrice had expected a decision. One way or the other. It had never occurred to her that she and Teddy and Cyrus and Ollie might go through all this—and actually succeed in freeing Rhona and the villagers—and still not know their status. It seemed terribly unfair. Just how many times did a witch have to face death before she was deemed worthy?

Beatrice opened her mouth to speak her mind, but Dr. Featherstone beat her to it.

"Have patience," the older witch said softly. "It will all be worth it, I promise you. Did you know that your name is already legend in Winter Wood?"

Her name was *legend*? Now Beatrice was too overcome to speak. But Teddy was not.

"When do we start the next test?" Teddy demanded.

"After you've rested," Dr. Featherstone said. "You're inexperienced in magic, so your powers will need some time to rejuvenate."

"How long?" Teddy went on stubbornly. "A day? A week?"

"Oh, my, no." Dr. Featherstone laughed uneasily at Teddy's intensity. "You'll go back to your families in the mortal world and the Executive Committee will let you know when the time is right."

Beatrice felt relieved—then guilty. Performing brave deeds was exhausting work, and she wanted nothing more than the comfort of her own bed. If they left early in the morning, she could still make it home for Halloween night. But even as she longed to return to her safe, familiar life, Beatrice couldn't forget that Rhona was counting on her.

At this point, Dr. Meadowmouse asked Dr. Featherstone to dance, and all the Institute witches wandered off to enjoy the party.

"We're supposed to go to the southern part of Bailiwick next," Teddy said. "What's the name of that place, Ollie?"

"Werewolf Close," Ollie said, and added, "You're obsessing, Teddy."

"So what?" she snapped. "I didn't get to show what I can do."

"Maybe we'll visit the werewolves over Winter Break," Cyrus said soothingly.

"That soon?" Beatrice asked. Winter Break was just around the corner.

Teddy eyed Beatrice shrewdly. "You're still not really into this, are you?"

"Not the way you are, no," Beatrice said defensively. "In fact, if it weren't for Bromwich and Rhona and her sisters, I wouldn't come back to the Witches' Sphere at all. I don't care if they *never* make me a Classical witch. I *like* being an Everyday witch."

Ollie and Cyrus laughed.

Even Teddy was smiling when she said, "Now where have I heard that before?"

"You know, it's Halloween Eve, and there's a party going on," Ollie said.

"Right," Cyrus agreed. "Let's forget about evil spells and sorcerers for tonight and have a good time."

Which was exactly what everyone else was doing. Beatrice took a sip of her phantom punch and sat back to observe the festivities. There were Birdella and Gus roasting apples over Fairarmfull's open mouth. Cayenne and Wooly Mittens were lapping up bowls of dragon's milk, and even Trembling Tom had ventured out from under the stairs and was gazing adoringly at Cayenne. The Rattlebones were playing a lively tune, and the ghosts were dancing across the field in the moonlight. Beatrice noticed with a start that Amarantha was out there dancing with one of them.

"Birdella," Beatrice called out, "who's that with Amarantha?"

"Odd Begley."

"The one that was haunting Skull House and driving Neva crazy?"

Birdella nodded and giggled. "But now he's got other things on his mind besides haunting, if you get what I mean."

Leopold Meadowmouse and Aura Featherstone were on the terrace dance floor cutting a rug, and Thaddeus Thigpin was dancing with Matilda Cronk—who didn't appear to be missing Roger at all. Neva was lighting jack-o'-lanterns with a point of her finger when suddenly she burst out with a traditional Halloween song. By the second verse, everyone had joined in.

> *Jack-o'-lanterns in a row,*
> *Our good wishes they do show.*
> *'Tis the best day of the year,*
> *When with friends we share good cheer.*
> *Happy, happy, happy, happy,*
> *Happy Halloween!*

Ollie poured Beatrice another cup of punch. "Would you like to dance later?" he asked.

"Sure," Beatrice said, and blushed.

It was then that she decided to stop fighting the inevitable. Someone, somewhere, had written in a ratty old book that Beatrice Bailey would try to be more than she had ever dreamed of being. Fair or not, that was the way things were. And she had to admit that it felt pretty good knowing that Rhona was free to come and go as she pleased, and that the people of Winter Wood no longer had to live in fear of Dally Rumpe. Beatrice couldn't take credit for all of that, but she might concede that she had had a little to do with it. She smiled, remembering Dr. Featherstone's words. *Your name is legend.*

Beatrice allowed herself a moment of pure vanity, basking in the memory of the villagers' homage whether it was deserved or not. Then she quickly came to her senses and steered herself back to reality—where she was nothing very special, just an Everyday witch. When the Witches' Executive Committee gave the word, she would try as hard as she could to break the rest of Dally Rumpe's spell. Meanwhile, Ollie had the right idea. It was nearly Halloween, and there was a party going on!

Beatrice raised her cup of punch to Ollie, Teddy, Cyrus, and Cayenne. "To good friends," she said.

"Good friends," the others chorused.

"And to whatever the future holds," Beatrice said happily. "So mote it be!"